"Stop! Police!"

The figure bending over Jillian jerked his head toward Luke, lifted his hand and fired a shot. The gunfire echoed around Luke as he crouched and fired back.

The suspect took off running.

Luke gave chase, heading toward the hiking trail. He stopped only for a moment to listen, pulled out his flashlight and shone it into the brush, not seeing anything.

Sirens wailed in the distance. His backup was on the way.

He needed to make sure Jillian was okay. He hurried down the trail to where she was sitting up but still on the ground.

"Is the shooting over with?" Her voice sounded wispy thin and weak.

He holstered his weapon. "Hopefully. Are you hurt?" Being careful not to shine the light into her eyes, he aimed his flashlight in her direction. She had only one shoe on.

She nodded and took in a jagged breath. "I guess they found me."

Ever since she found the Nancy Drew books with the pink covers in the country school library, **Sharon Dunn** has loved mystery and suspense. In 2014, she lost her beloved husband of nearly twenty-seven years to cancer. She has three grown children. When she is not writing, she enjoys reading, sewing and walks. She loves to hear from readers. You can contact her via her website at www.sharondunnbooks.net.

Books by Sharon Dunn

Love Inspired Suspense

Visit the Author Profile page at LoveInspired.com for more titles.

TARGETED MONTANA WITNESS

SHARON DUNN

LOVE INSPIRED SUSPENSE
INSPIRATIONAL ROMANCE

LOVE INSPIRED® SUSPENSE

INSPIRATIONAL ROMANCE

ISBN-13: 978-1-335-63878-6

Targeted Montana Witness

Recycling programs
for this product may
not exist in your area.

Love Inspired
22 Adelaide St. West, 41st Floor
Toronto, Ontario M5H 4E3, Canada
www.LoveInspired.com

Printed in Lithuania

MIX
Paper | Supporting
responsible forestry
FSC® C021394

Behold I will do a new thing;
now it shall spring forth; shall ye not know it?
—*Isaiah* 43:19

As always, this book is dedicated to my readers,
who keep me encouraged and writing.

ONE

With a heavy sigh, Jillian Welch clicked on her vacuum and ran it over the carpet of the offices she cleaned six nights a week. She'd work seven nights a week if they'd give her the hours. The night off was always a struggle. For someone with insomnia, this job was ideal. But it was a far cry from what she used to do as an ER nurse. She missed the excitement and being a part of a team that saved lives. A sadness settled around her. Who she used to be was behind a locked door that could never be opened again.

She turned off the vacuum and walked a few feet to pick up the coffee she always bought on her way into work. The liquid tasted sweet on her tongue, though it was already lukewarm. Stopping at the Coffee Experience hut was part of her nighttime routine. And routines and schedules helped her get through her day.

Her phone rang as she leaned over to wind up the vacuum cord. She pulled it from her pocket and stared at the screen. An unknown number. Who would be calling her at this time of night? She didn't know that many people in the small Montana town where she lived. Jillian pressed the connect button and drew the phone closer to her face.

"Hello?"

A gravelly male voice came across the line. "I know who you really are."

Jillian's throat went dry as she was sucked back into the past. She reached out toward the wall to steady herself. Three years ago, she'd testified against her fiancé's killer, a hitman for the New Jersey mafia. The trial had landed the hitman in prison and had led to the jailing of the mafia boss who'd hired him. The hitman, Gordon Burnett, had threatened Jillian's life as he was dragged from the courtroom. Knowing that people who worked for the mafia had lots of connections and usually made good on threats of revenge had compelled her into witness protection. She'd left her old life behind and moved across the country to Spring Meadow, Montana.

Jillian stared at her phone screen. Had the mafia found her anyway?

Her heart pounded as she cleared her throat. "Who…who is this?"

The moment stretched out, and she could hear

the man breathing. Her heartbeat drummed in her ears. He disconnected.

Paralyzed with fear, she stared at the phone.

Call for help.

Her hands were shaking as she scrolled through her contacts. Only one person in this town knew who she really was. Though a US marshal was her contact with the program, it was standard practice to inform one person in local law enforcement of her true identity if she needed immediate assistance for any reason.

She'd met Sheriff Luke Mayfair only once. At a café several towns over. Marshal Stiller, her contact in the program, had introduced them. He wasn't much older than she was, with windswept blond hair and intense brown eyes. He came across as professional but aloof. His suggestion that her Jersey accent made her stand out like a sore thumb had fed the fear about being found. He seemed oblivious to how the comment had affected her. All the same, she'd put effort into learning to talk as if she'd been born and raised in the West.

Since then, she and Luke had had very little interaction, not more than a nod and a hello when they met on a downtown street. But now she needed his help.

She pressed his number.

A warm baritone voice came across the line.

"Hello, Jillian." He sounded surprised or as if his greeting had a question mark at the end of it.

No time for small talk. "I'm at work. I just got a very scary phone call from a man. Someone saying they knew who I was." Jillian's life was built on secrets, and shortly after she moved to Spring Meadow, she'd created one more. There was something about her that not even Marshal Stiller or the sheriff knew. Could that be the cause of the disturbing phone call?

"Did you recognize the voice? Did he identify himself in any way?"

Wishing her heart wasn't beating so fast, she gripped the phone tighter. "He only said that one sentence and then hung up."

"Are you alone in the building?"

Her breath caught. Did the sheriff think the man might be close?

"Yes. I'm here alone." She walked over to the third-story window that looked out on the parking lot where her car was. Then she saw it. Another car was in the lot. The sound of the elevator drew her attention back inside. All the air left her lungs. Her words came out in a hoarse whisper. "He's here."

She could barely hear Sheriff Mayfair's voice as she ran toward the stairwell. He said something about being on his way. Behind her, the elevator doors slid open. She wouldn't make it to the stairs without being spotted. She darted into the closest open door, a dark office. The desk, which was more like a glass table, would not provide a place to hide. She slipped behind a plant stand in the corner of the room. The stand was tall enough that it hid her whole body if she scrunched down and pressed her arms close to her sides. She had a limited view of the room if she peered between the pots.

Her heartbeat thrummed in her ears in time to the approaching footsteps. Then the silence fell around her like a smothering blanket. The man was standing on the threshold of the office she was in. His knees cracked when he shifted his weight. Beads of sweat formed on her forehead. Had he seen her go in here or was he searching each office?

She squeezed her eyes shut and prayed that he would leave.

A brushing noise told her he was fumbling for the light switch. He grunted.

She winced as a bright beam came on and was swung around the room. He had a flashlight. She could hear his footsteps on the carpet. She bent her neck, trying to see where he was. The man stepped toward her hiding place. He was nearly on top of her, but his back was turned. His attention was on something across the room where he was pointing the light. If he turned around, and aimed the flashlight her way, she would have only seconds before he spotted her. She pushed on the plant stand, toppling the heavy pots and shattering the pottery in a cacophony of noise.

Groans of pain told her she'd hit her target. The flashlight rolled across the floor.

She ran toward the open door and the dimly lit main office area where the carrels and office equipment were.

A cold intense grip tightened around her ankle. She screamed, falling to the floor as he yanked. Before her body collided with the carpet, she twisted around, so she landed on her bottom instead of her stomach. When she kicked her leg, his grasp slipped. She'd freed herself but lost her shoe in the process.

She flipped over and pushed herself to her feet.

The man grabbed her shirttails from behind. She reached for the nearest object on the desk, which turned out to be some sort of metal statue that she pummeled the attacker with, hitting his shoulder and head until he let go.

Still holding the object, she turned and sprinted toward the threshold. Her assault had disabled the man enough that it bought her precious seconds of time.

Once in the main area, she clicked the switch that controlled all the lights in this part of the office. Her advantage was that she knew the layout of this place. As the room went dark, she pressed against a wall and eased toward the door of the stairwell. She could hear her assailant stomping and stumbling across the carpet, groaning when he bumped into something.

"You can't hide any longer." His voice was filled with menace.

Her breath caught as she reached out toward the door to the stairwell. Opening it would clue her attacker as to where she was.

A light arced in the darkness. He'd gone back and found his flashlight.

Knowing she had only seconds to flee, she eased the door open a couple of inches and side-stepped onto the landing. The concrete was cold on her shoeless foot. The stairwell was lit with a single bulb. She raced down, expecting the door above her to swing open at any moment.

She hesitated at the second-floor landing, wondering if she should find a hiding place or try to get to her car. There hadn't been time for Sheriff Mayfair to say how far away he was. Hiding might get her killed. She'd dropped her phone in the struggle to get away. She couldn't call him to find out. Her car keys were in her pocket. Waiting around for the sheriff to show up could cost her her life.

Still not hearing any indication that she'd been followed, Jillian hurried down to the first floor, which was a labyrinth of small offices for separate businesses. The attacker may have taken the elevator down.

She sprinted toward the doors that led to the parking lot.

She stopped momentarily, drawing her keys out and separating them so the one that would start her car would be quickly accessible. Then she pushed open the door, still gripping the statue in case she needed to use it as a weapon again stepping out into the chill September night.

She sprinted across the concrete to her car. Once there, she lifted her head but didn't see or hear anything. The other car was still across the lot.

She swung open the door and got behind the wheel, twisting the key in the ignition as she grabbed her seat belt. She clicked on the headlights and drove toward the exit.

Suddenly, the car jolted forward with an intensity that had her jaw clenching. Metal crunched against metal as the other car hit her from behind. She pressed the gas and sped toward the dark street.

Her whole body felt like it was being shaken from the inside. A large field and a park surrounded by a hiking trail separated the office building from the rest of town. She pressed the accelerator as she drove up the hill toward the lights of an apartment complex and, beyond that, a strip mall.

When she checked the rearview mirror, lights filled her field of vision. She heard the roar of an engine right before the other car impacted with her back bumper. Her body lurched forward and then back as if she were a rag doll.

When she drew her attention to the windshield, she had view of the field as she rolled through it. The car slammed her from behind two more times before she came to a stop. Her engine was no longer running.

With its lights still on, the other car remained behind her.

She had to get away.

Fighting off dizziness, she lifted a trembling hand to turn the key in the ignition.

Her car door burst open. She reached for the metal statue on the passenger seat. The attacker hit her hard across the jaw, and the blow stunned her for a moment as the pain vibrated through her head.

Confined by the seat belt, she swung the statue hitting the attacker's arms twice before he yanked the weapon out of her hands and tossed it away.

The man reached across her lap and undid her seat belt. She hit his head and shoulders with her fists, but it had no effect on him. He grabbed her by the shoulders and pulled her from the car.

"Now I've got you," he said.

His face was very close to hers. The man was wearing a ski mask.

She tried to pry his fingers off her as he dragged her toward his car, which he'd left running.

She planted her feet and clawed at his hands, trying to gain some control. When his grip released, she took off running.

He grabbed her from behind and pushed her to the ground. Her stomach pressed against the hard earth, knocking the wind out of her. *Please, God, I don't want to die.*

"You're not getting away from me." His voice was filled with menace as he pulled out a gun.

Terror sliced her to the bone.

When he noticed the two cars off the road in a nearby field, Sheriff Luke Mayfair knew something was amiss. He slowed his patrol vehicle, and as he drew closer, he saw that the car farther away was Jillian's. He'd been heading to her office building to find her, but it seemed she'd gotten away already—and run into trouble while trying to make an escape. After calling for backup, he jumped out with his weapon drawn.

The first car sitting at an angle a few yards from the street was still running with its lights on. Aiming his gun at the driver's side window, he peered inside. Empty.

Noise drew his attention deeper into the field. He stalked forward. Just beyond Jillian's front bumper, he saw the silhouettes of two people in a struggle, one on the ground and the other bent over her.

"Stop, police!"

The bent-over figure jerked his head toward Luke, lifted his hand and fired a shot in Luke's direction. Luke crouched immediately as gunfire echoed around him. He fired back.

The suspect took off running.

Luke gave chase as he headed toward the tall bushes that surrounded the hiking trail. Once on the trail, Luke stopped for a moment to listen. The pounding of footsteps told him the suspect was on the move. Luke wasn't far behind.

Aware that the man was armed, he sprinted toward the noise. The suspect wouldn't be able to get off a shot unless he stopped and turned around. Even then, he'd be shooting in the dark.

Luke rounded two switchbacks on the trail. Hearing no more telltale noise, he slowed. He still had his weapon ready but feared the suspect might be hiding in order to shoot at Luke unawares. If this man was mafia, sent to silence Jillian, he was no doubt incredibly dangerous.

Luke didn't know Jillian well but had gotten a

summary of her case file. He hadn't spoken to her since Marshal Stiller introduced them years ago, and while he'd been happy to do his duty to help while she was in the program, years had passed incident-free since she'd come to Montana. Her phone call tonight had taken him by surprise. He pulled his flashlight and shone it in the brush but didn't see anything.

Sirens wailed in the distance. His backup was on the way.

Jillian had been moving but was still on the ground when he'd run past her. He needed to make sure she was okay.

He hurried up the trail and out into the open.

Flashing lights indicated that support had arrived. The two deputies, a man and a woman, got out of a single patrol car and both had pulled their guns.

Luke pointed at the trail, yelling, "Suspect went that way. He's armed. One of you take the path on foot. The other circle around in the vehicle. That trail comes out somewhere. I'll stay with the victim."

Deputy Chris Tyler, his new hire, sprinted toward where Luke had indicated while Deputy Angie Walters ran back to the patrol car. Luke rushed over to where the victim was sitting up but still on the ground. Jillian's light brown hair had come lose from the ponytail she usually wore it in. He remembered being intrigued by her dark eyes and the unique shade of her hair when they'd met. It was pretty.

"Is the shooting over with?" Her head was bent and her voice sounded wispy, thin and weak.

He holstered his weapon. "Hopefully. Are you hurt? Do you think you can get up?" He pulled his flashlight off his utility belt. Being careful not to shine the light in her eyes, he aimed it in her direction. She had only one shoe on.

She nodded and took in a jagged breath. "I think so."

He helped her get to her feet. "It's all right. I've got you."

She moaned in pain.

Even in the dark, he could see scratches on her face. "Let's get you to the hospital to be checked out."

She swayed and her knees buckled. He braced his arm across her back to steady her.

"I hope your deputies catch him." She sighed.

"Me too." He escorted her to his patrol car, then moved to open the passenger side door for her. Light from inside the cab revealed a bruise on her jaw. Anger flared in him at what she'd gone through tonight. He'd do everything in his power to catch this guy. He waited until she was secure in the vehicle before running around to the driver's side.

When he got behind the wheel, she pressed her head against the seat back. Her eyes were closed. "I guess they found me, Luke."

He noted the agony that undergirded the softness of her voice. He'd lived his whole life in this county. He could not imagine what it would be like to uproot and leave behind everyone and everything you knew. Now it looked like she was going to have to do it again. Her comment made him wonder if she'd spent the whole time here looking over her shoulder, wondering when the people who wanted revenge would come after her. Witness protection was no easy way to live.

"It looks that way," he said.

No one else in this town knew what she'd been through. Their interaction had been minimal since they'd met. A hello and nod when their paths crossed in public places. She'd lost her fiancé to violence. To a degree, Luke understood about that kind of loss. The woman he'd been engaged to had died in a car accident when they were both twenty. He and Maria had known each other since the fourth grade, and her death had torn a chasm through his psyche. He couldn't imagine ever loving anyone else. Why risk such catastrophic loss again?

Even though Jillian had taken his advice and worked on covering the Jersey accent, it looked like she'd been found anyway.

He'd noticed her from a distance when he saw her around town. Any time there was a child or an old person on the sidewalk, she stopped to interact with them. She seemed to have compassion for the vulnerable.

Luke started his vehicle, turned back onto the road and headed toward the hospital.

Jillian crossed her arms over her middle and slumped forward. "I'm pretty sure he was trying to drag me back to his car so he could find an out-of-the-way place to shoot me. Leave me where the body wouldn't be found right away."

The attack sounded pretty brutal. Luke wanted to say something to comfort her. "You're safe now." He drove toward the lights of the town, stopping at the nearly dark strip mall and turning up the hill to the hospital.

"Am I?"

"What I meant was in this patrol car with me, you're not likely to be attacked again." There was nothing he could say to take away what had happened. Catching the attacker would end her fear. "Did you get a look at the guy?"

She shook her head. "I saw that he had on a ski mask when he pulled me from the car."

"And he said, 'I know who you are'? That's all he said?"

"He didn't talk much. He said a few other things to me when he came after me in the field.

His voice was kind of gruff." Jillian took audible breaths between each sentence. She was either in distress or needed to be checked out medically. They were nearly at the hospital.

"I guess there's only one possibility of who would say something like that," he said.

She shifted in her seat and looked away. She ran her fingers through her hair. "Yes, I guess." She seemed to be avoiding eye contact. Was there something she wasn't telling him?

He had more questions, but it was clear she was in no condition to answer them just yet. "You'll have to get in touch with Marshal Stiller."

She nodded but then shook her head. "I don't have my phone. I dropped it when that guy came after me." Her voice wavered.

Luke could tell that she was reliving the attack and all the terror connected with it. "It's all right. We'll deal with this one step at a time. Let's focus on making sure you're okay physically."

She rested her palm on her chest and nodded. "Yes, that's what we need to do."

He pulled into the hospital parking lot by the ER entrance. His radio crackled and he lifted it. "Did you catch the suspect?"

Deputy Walters's voice came across the line. She sounded out of breath. "Deputy Tyler and I met up where the trail connects with the road.

We both searched on foot at that point. No sign of him. We think he may have hitched a ride."

In Luke's peripheral vision, he watched Jillian's body crumple as she let out a heavy sigh.

He spoke into the radio. "But you're not sure?"

"We'll keep searching. If he's still on foot, we might be able to catch him," said Deputy Walters.

"Keep me in the loop," Luke replied. "He left his car behind. If you could check the name on the registration, it might give us a place to start. Then I'll make arrangements for it to go to the state crime lab."

"Ten-four," Deputy Walters replied.

Luke put the radio back in its slot.

Jillian's lips were drawn into a pensive line. "He's still out there."

Luke nodded. "I'll stay with you until you contact Marshal Stiller and we figure out what the next step is."

Once they were inside the ER, he waited with her until a nurse came to take her to an exam room. He found a chair and sat outside it.

His shoulder radio crackled again. He turned his head and clicked the talk button. "Go ahead."

"It's Walters. We got a problem." Her voice was crisp and forceful.

He tensed. "What's going on?"

"The car isn't here anymore. He must have doubled back or been hiding close by."

Luke ground his teeth together. "So, he's mobile?"

"Looks that way."

Luke exhaled his frustration. "You can still keep an eye out for the car while you're on shift. You got a look at it, didn't you?" Angie had been a deputy longer than he'd been the sheriff. He could always count on her top-notch observational skills.

"Late model SUV, probably early 2000s. Dark in color," she said.

He nodded. "Why don't you and Deputy Tyler keep looking until you get another call? I'm staying close to the victim for now."

"You think he might come after her again? Why is that—any idea who he is?"

He couldn't answer that question without revealing that Jillian was in witness protection. "It's just a precaution."

"Do you know why Jillian was attacked in the first place?"

It was good police work for Deputy Walters to ask for details, but he had to be careful not to reveal too much. "I'm hoping she can answer some questions once she feels up to it."

After signing off with Angie, Luke rose to his feet and paced toward a window that looked out on the parking lot.

If the suspect had been hiding close by and

watching, it would have been easy enough to see which way Luke's patrol car had turned and guess at where he was headed with Jillian. They could have been followed to the hospital.

Her life certainly had been turned upside down yet again. He wondered why she'd seemed cagey when he concluded that someone connected to her past was after her. Was there some other reason she would be attacked like that?

He watched several cars turn off the street and drive toward the parking spaces close to the ER entrance. Almost involuntarily, his hand hovered over the holstered gun on his hip. The guy was still out there waiting for another chance to come after Jillian. And when he did, Luke would be ready.

TWO

Though the nurse practitioner had checked her out and given her the okay to go, the tension that threaded through Jillian's torso had not subsided. It wasn't just about the attack and knowing that the man who'd come after her was still out there.

She'd kept a piece of information from Luke that might be important. There was another possibility for someone saying, "I know who you are."

Only Luke knew why she'd been put in witness protection. He knew who she used to be. But no one in this town knew her other secret. When she'd first been placed in the program three years ago, the sense of being untethered from any kind of community or identity had overwhelmed her.

She could be with people, but she could never truly be herself. She had friends she met for coffee or to grab dinner. But it always felt like there was a chasm between her and the other person, like she was wearing a mask.

To deal with the insomnia, she'd started a podcast called *Voice in the Night*. She read Scripture, played relaxing music and spoke words of comfort to other people who couldn't sleep. She felt like she was helping people, like when she'd been a nurse back in Jersey, and in an odd way, the podcast had eased her sense of separation from other people. Though she never used her name on the show, she felt like she could take the mask off. She had regular listeners, and judging from the comments, what she did helped people get through their own sleepless nights.

From the start, she knew that doing the podcast held a degree of risk. But so did the depression that had plagued her ever since she'd entered the program. That at least had lifted shortly after her first show.

She'd taken every precaution to hide who she was and not be found. Her show was audio only. Nowhere on the places people could link to the program did her picture appear. Purging herself of her Jersey accent meant people wouldn't even be able to guess where she was from. The show had in fact been a good place to practice speaking without the accent.

Twice in the last week though, she'd found gifts, a stuffed animal and a bracelet, once on the hood of her car and once on her doorstep. There was an older woman at church who liked to leave anonymous presents for people. Jillian had wanted to believe that was who the gifts were from. Now she wasn't so sure.

Was it possible someone who was deeply disturbed listened to the show and had figured out who she was and where she lived? Had he come to town to attack her at work?

Luke stepped into the room holding his cowboy hat, spinning it in his hands. His honey-colored hair, which grew past his ears and had a shaggy look to it, didn't quite fit with the pristine appearance of his uniform. He looked more like he ought to be running toward the ocean with a surfboard under his arm.

Though he always seemed guarded and overly professional, she'd thought he was a handsome man the first time she'd seen him at the café. But she'd squelched any feelings of attraction from the moment they'd met. Her past told her that where men were concerned, she was not a very good judge of character.

Though her fiancé had presented himself as a successful businessman who ran several pizza places, Gregory had not been an innocent victim of a mafia hit. The mob's money had been laundered through his pizza parlors, and he'd been killed for skimming.

The whole relationship had been a lie. She was an intelligent educated woman. How could she not have seen him for who he was? She didn't trust herself anymore where men were concerned. Maybe she'd been vulnerable to Gregory's charm because she'd thought with him, she'd have a family again. She was an only child and both of her parents had died.

Luke stepped toward the exam table. "Doc says you can go."

"Yes, no concussion, nothing broken, just some cuts and bruises." She touched her jaw where it was sore from being hit.

He placed his hat back on his head. "So, are you ready to call the marshal?"

Guilt pricked the corners of her conscience. She had to tell Luke about the podcast, but she needed to find the right moment. "I'd like to go get my phone back at the office and stop to see if my car is drivable. That way I can make the call from my house so there's no danger of being overheard."

Luke nodded. "That's a smart idea. Let's do that then."

"The nurse gave me some slippers to wear since I lost my shoe. I think we can find that too," she said.

The sun was just coming up when they stepped out into the hospital parking lot. Luke stayed close to her, and she noticed that his gaze bounced through the whole parking lot.

His hypervigilance put her nerves on edge. "Your deputy said that they thought the attacker had hitched a ride or was still on foot…"

He kept walking. "She radioed me when you were in the exam room. It looks like he came back and got his car while they were out searching for him on the trail." They were at Luke's patrol vehicle. He opened the passenger side door for her.

A tingling chill washed over her skin. She could not purge the fear from her voice. "Oh, I see." The attacker could get around that much faster in a car. He might even have followed them to the hospital.

Luke rested his hand on her shoulder. "I'll stay with you until he's caught, or the marshal can get you relocated to a safe place."

His assurance brought her comfort but didn't ease any of the tension from her body. She climbed into the passenger seat.

Luke drove her to her car. The back bumper was hanging by a thread, but the car started up fine. He followed her to the office building. Except for their vehicles, the parking lot was empty.

He kept in step with her as they headed to the front doors. "If you feel up to it, it might be good if you walked me through what happened."

The suggestion made her tense up and stutter in her step.

He touched her arm and spoke softly. "Anything you can remember about the suspect would be helpful."

She pressed in the four-digit code, and the door buzzed open. "I understand that." She was pretty sure the entrance doors had been locked when she'd been working on the third floor. The man who attacked her must have bypassed the security system…or known the code. That thought had her more nervous. Once inside, she turned to face Luke. She hadn't noticed before that his brown eyes had gold flecks in them, making them luminescent. "I told you I never saw his face."

"You're more likely to remember accurately if you try to recall what happened sooner rather than later. Even what he was wearing might be helpful," he said. "Tattoos on his arms or chest. Did he wear rings or a distinct necklace?"

She shook her head. "It all happened so fast. I think he was dressed in dark colors." Luke was only trying to do his job, but even being back in this building put her on edge. Trying to picture the man who had attacked her made it hard to get a deep breath. "I just want to go up and find my phone and shoe and gather up my cleaning supplies."

By the time the elevator doors to the third floor opened up for them, her heart was thudding in her chest. A patina of sweat had formed on her forehead.

Luke leaned closer to her. "I know this isn't easy. It might even be bringing back what you witnessed in New Jersey."

They stepped out onto the carpeted area. There was a lump in her throat when she tried to speak. "Yes, it has caused a bit of PTSD."

The one blessing in all this was that Luke knew the level of violence she'd witnessed in New Jersey. She was so grateful that he understood how the recent attack would cause dark memories to rise to the surface.

She found her phone just outside the office where she'd hidden. The shoe was inside the office.

Luke stopped her as she reached to pick it up. "Wait. It might have his fingerprints on it. We can't get a full forensics team in here without calling attention to you being in WITSEC. But I can get some info and pass it on to the marshal's office."

An image flashed in her mind. She shook her head. "He was wearing gloves."

"That's a helpful detail. Sounds like a little planning went into this whole thing."

Luke helped her pick up some of the broken pottery from the plant stand. She'd have to give the office manager an explanation as to what had happened and offer to pay for the damage.

As she discarded the shards of pottery, the memories of what happened in New Jersey bombarded her. Entering the closed pizza parlor on a rainy night and hearing the raised voices in the kitchen. Gregory shouting as she approached the swinging doors, then the gunshots that sent her sprinting for the counter. She'd slipped behind a dessert display case when the hitman stomped through the eating area but had had a clear view of him through the glass.

She shuddered and tossed more of the broken pottery in the garbage.

Luke carried her vacuum, and she grabbed the caddy filled with rags and detergents. They took the elevator down before stepping outside into the warmth of morning light.

As she drove toward her home, Luke stayed close behind her in the patrol vehicle. Something about seeing him in the rearview mirror eased the tension in her body. All the same, she still found herself scanning the side streets and approaching cars.

She passed through a light that had just turned yellow. She slowed down. Luke was left waiting at the light. There was hardly any traffic at this hour. A dark-colored car was behind her. She hadn't even seen it turn onto the street. The car loomed close to hers. Though the attack had happened in the dark, this car looked a lot like the one the assailant had been driving.

Her heart pounded. Luke was still stuck at the light behind her, and the light up ahead turned red. She pressed the brake. The car behind her was not slowing down. As it sped ever closer to her bumper, she accelerated and turned suddenly onto a side street to avoid being hit.

The car turned and followed her.

She scanned the area looking for a place where she might be in the safety of people. This was a street with offices that were still closed.

The other car zoomed toward her and smashed her bumper. The impact jarred her and caused her head to snap back and forward again. She veered up on the sidewalk and yanked the wheel to get back onto the street.

This time the car was coming at her from the side.

She pressed the gas. The other car hit her back bumper hard again, causing it to fishtail. She kept her foot on the accelerator.

In the distance, she heard a siren. Luke had seen what had happened.

She turned her head, hoping to see the driver. The flash of an image told her nothing but that the driver was male. His hat covered his hair and part of his face. Her attacker backed up and sped away, then turned down another side street.

She pulled over, shaking uncontrollably. Seconds later, Luke was opening her door. He pressed a warm hand on her cheek.

"It's all right. Which way did he go? I can call it in. Maybe we can catch him."

She pointed with a trembling finger. "Up Cleveland Street."

Her car door remained open. She could hear Luke as he spoke on his radio. She unclicked the seat belt and stepped out. She thought she might be sick. Her stomach roiled and her knees were weak.

Luke was beside her. He gathered her into his arms. "It's okay. I've got you."

He held her for a long moment until the nausea passed and she calmed down. "Thank you. I think I can make it home now."

His gaze was intense as they stood close together on the empty street. "Maybe we should head back to the hospital."

"Please, I'm fine. I just want to go home." Tears welled in her eyes. Home where it was safe.

He nodded. "Is your car drivable?"

"I think so." She turned back toward the open driver's side door.

Luke steadied her by cupping a hand under her elbow. He waited on the street until she was buckled in and had closed her door. She turned the key in the ignition. The car started. She gave him a nod and a thumbs-up.

His attentiveness smoothed over her frayed nerves, and the fear that played at the corners of her mind.

He walked back to his car. She watched the side-view mirror, waiting until he was in his patrol car before pulling out onto the street.

The sight of her little house coming into view gave her comfort. She parked on the street by her house. Luke parked right behind her.

Once she saw he was out of his car, she pushed her door open, and he escorted her up to her doorstep. She stopped at the base of the stairs. A pot of flowers rested on the stoop.

"Looks like you have a present," he said.

Her head buzzed as she reached down, picked up the pot and pulled out the card.

I cared about you. Your voice gave me comfort. But you ignored me. You will pay.

Quickly, she folded the card into her palm as Luke reached out for the pot. "Here, let me hold that so you can open the door."

She thought her knees might buckle. By the time she'd put the key in the lock and opened the door, she was having trouble getting a deep breath.

As soon as she opened the door, her cat emerged from the kitchen and trotted toward her. When the ginger tabby meowed, the warm greeting lifted some of the agitation she was feeling. She reached down to stroke the feline's back. "Hey, Marmy."

Even though she was facing away from him, she could feel the weight of Luke's gaze. "Marmy?"

"Short for Marmalade." Jillian straightened up and turned to where Luke stood on the threshold still holding the flowerpot. Morning light gave his skin a soft glow.

She pointed at the entryway table. "You can just set the flowers down there."

The furrow between his brows communicated confusion. "Jillian, what's going on?"

She crumpled the card in her hand as a tightness spread through her chest. No more waiting for the right moment. It had to be now. She took in a breath. "I have something to tell you."

Luke stepped toward Jillian. Her face blanched as she bit her lower lip, which caused the muscles in his neck to knot up in response. Something was wrong. His eyes searched hers as they stood close together in the narrow entryway.

"What is it?" he asked

She averted her gaze and ran her fingers through her long hair. "The man who came after me is probably not connected to the case I testi-fied in."

"Okay…do you want to explain?"

She turned away from Luke and stared at the ground. "I may have done a foolish thing. I know when Marshal Stiller briefed me, he said not to do anything that might get me in the news or draw attention to myself. He advised me to keep a low profile and do a job where I was invisible."

Luke shifted his weight and shook his head. "I still don't understand."

"Maybe I can show you." She walked through the living room down a hallway into a bedroom. She stepped toward what he assumed was a closet hidden by a curtain.

She pulled back the curtain to reveal a table where a microphone and two laptops sat, along with a Bible.

He took his cowboy hat off and twisted it in his hands. Something he always did when he was nervous. "You do some sort of broadcast?"

"It's audio only. I took enormous precautions that no one would connect the podcast to me even under my new last name."

Why did it feel like both of them were sink-ing in quicksand? This was not good. "I'm sure the marshal isn't going to be happy about this."

She pressed her back against the wall. "I know it wasn't the smartest thing to do, but when I first moved here, I almost couldn't cope. The podcast gave me a chance to practice talking without an accent. But there's a bigger reason. You have no idea what it was like to be dropped into a world where I didn't know anyone. I needed to feel useful on my night off instead of pacing the floor because I couldn't sleep. I wanted to find a way to connect with people on a deep level."

He kept his ire at bay. Being upset with her wouldn't fix anything. "I get that, but couldn't you just volunteer at the senior citizens center?"

"They don't keep the same hours that I do. If you only knew what a struggle it was in the early days when I first came here. The podcast filled a need. It made me feel less lonely. I felt like I could truly be myself. Not the pretend person from a WITSEC file." Tears rimmed her eyes and then flowed down her cheeks.

He felt a tug at his heart. He wanted to wipe those tears away. He had no idea what she'd been going through in the three years since she'd been placed here. He'd seen only the side of herself she presented in public. Until now, he hadn't fathomed how hard an adjustment it had been for her.

She still held the note in her tightly fisted hand. "So, the flowers were from someone who knows about the show?" He leaned toward her. "Can I see what he wrote?"

She lifted her hand and turned it over. He

reached out to cup underneath her hand and bend the fingers open. Her skin had a silky softness to it.

A shockwave surged through him when he read the note. "Well, that makes it pretty clear. He mentions your voice. This is a threat to your safety regardless. You still need to call the marshal. I'll stay with you for now."

She closed her eyes and remained with her back pressed against the wall. "I don't want to be relocated. I'd don't want to change my last name again, get a different job, take on another persona with a fictional past. It was hard enough the first time." She opened her eyes. "I don't like keeping secrets from people."

The pained look on her face shot right through him. Fueled by fear about the future, her mind must be going a hundred miles an hour. "Let's just take this one step at a time."

"I know I messed up. I understand how serious the threat to my life is. I do." She swiped at her eyes. "Do you know what's it like to hide who you really are from people?"

He wasn't sure how to answer that. "It's what you have to do to stay alive, Jillian." He glanced around the sparsely furnished room noticing a lump in the bedspread. The lump moved a little bit.

"That's my other cat, George. He's the opposite of Marmy. He hides when strangers come into the house."

Luke nodded. "Why don't we go sit down in the living room?" If nothing else, George would have his space back.

She pushed herself off the wall, drawing the curtain shut on her little recording studio before moving toward the door. He followed her back down the hallway. Jillian plunked down on the love seat. Her eyes still had an unfocused quality.

More than once in his career, he'd dealt with a distraught victim who'd become paralyzed by the trauma they'd been through. Jillian had that same look and hunched posture. She'd been through a lot, not just tonight but all that had gone down three years ago.

He stepped into her kitchen, opening several cupboards before he found a glass. He ran some water from the tap and took the glass over to her.

"Thank you." She took a sip of the water and set it on a side table.

Though the phone call had to be made, he first needed to bring her back to the present and help her relax. He glanced around the tiny living room. "You've made a cozy little space here."

She lifted her head and glanced at pictures on the walls and furniture. "Mostly stuff I found at thrift stores and estate sales." She pointed out a lamp and a painting telling the story of how she'd found them.

The distraction had worked. Her shoulders, which had been all but touching her ears, eased down as she shared.

After giving her another moment, he asked, "Are you ready to make that call?"

She nodded and pulled her phone out. "I'm afraid of what he's going to say." Her gaze moved from her phone to his face. "I don't think I have it in me to start all over again...to become invisible."

Invisible... He actually understood that, but in a different way. He was the youngest son in a farming family. It was his older brother, Matt, who had been given control of the land when their father died. Luke's opinion about what direction the farm should go didn't seem to matter. The whole family still lived on the property on the outskirts of town, and Luke gave suggestions where he could. He didn't need to get into any of that with Jillian. Getting that personal wouldn't be helpful. But he wondered why he even thought about wanting to share that with her. Something about her made him want to let his guard down. He thought about what she'd said about her podcast and could suddenly understand why people might find comfort in it. Listening to her and feeling a connection. "I'll sit with you while you make that call, or I can leave the room. Whatever would be most helpful."

"You should probably hear what the marshal has to say." She lifted the phone and pressed in the number. He knew the number wasn't one she kept in her contacts, even with an ambiguous name attached to it. At their meeting, the marshal had explained that Jillian had memorized it for her protection, and if she ever needed to reach him from a phone that wasn't hers.

Luke tensed as the phone rang three times. As they waited, his eye caught on the typed note once more. The threat to Jillian was unmistakable.

You will pay.

THREE

The phone rang a fourth time. Marshal Stiller's voice came across the line. "Jillian?"

Luke visibly relaxed. She was seeing a different side to him than the initial impression she'd gotten. At that first meeting he'd come across as a cold fish with no comprehension that what he said affected other people's feelings.

Now he seemed much more caring.

She took in a breath. "Marshal Stiller, I have a problem. I'm here in my house with Sheriff Mayfair."

"Has there been a breach in your identity?" Stiller asked.

"Not exactly." Her throat had gone tight. She explained about the podcast, finishing by sharing the note that Luke handed back to her.

There was a brief pause before the marshal said, "Mention of your voice does suggest this is connected to the podcast, but that attack at your place of work and then on the road sounds like his intent was to kill you."

Luke leaned toward the phone, so their heads were very close together. "Maybe the motive was kidnapping. He had a gun but didn't use it on her. When I arrived on the scene, he shot at me."

Jillian hadn't thought of that. "He did try to drag me to his car at first, but I got away." At the time, she'd thought the man wanted to kill her because she'd assumed he was connected to what had happened back east. "At first, I thought he was trying to get me to the car so he could take me somewhere secluded before he killed me." She shuddered at the idea. But if this was the work of a podcast stalker, could his aim have been to abduct her? If Luke hadn't shown up when he did, there was no telling what would've happened.

The marshal's commanding voice filled the room. "In any case, even if the source of the attack isn't connected to the man you put in prison, given what has happened, I think we need to look into moving you."

Jillian thought she might cry. "Please, I don't want to start over again. If we can catch this guy, I can stay here, can't I?"

The silence on the other end of the line made Jillian nervous. She glanced at Luke.

Marshal Stiller spoke up. "It will take a while to get the paperwork in place for a new identity and line up secure transport. Luke, can you stay close to Jillian until then?"

That seemed to be the marshal's version of a compromise.

"I'll do my best," Luke said. "If we could bring this guy in, Jillian could stay here in Spring Meadow, couldn't she?"

She appreciated that he had restated the question Marshal Stiller hadn't yet answered. Being stripped of the life she'd built here would be devastating. Luke seemed to understand that.

"The decision is always yours, Jillian," said Marshal Stiller. "You can leave the program all together and even go back to your old life if you choose. Others have done that. My job is to make sure you understand the risks."

Her mind reeled with the choices she had before her. "I know I can't go back to New Jersey. I want the protection the program gives me, but I don't want to start all over."

A silence hung in the air. Luke scooted to the edge of the chair while Jillian held the phone in her palm. Their heads were nearly touching now, and she could smell his aftershave. A light woodsy scent.

"I think we can catch this guy," said Luke. "Give my deputies and me a few days."

"Let's leave it there for now," said the marshal.

"One thing I do know, Jillian—you need to quit that podcast."

Sadness washed over her, but she understood. "Yes, I know."

"Luke, can you make sure she has some kind of protection at all times? Let me know if there's anything I can do in helping with the investigation."

"Sure, I can do that," Luke responded.

"Jillian, I would appreciate if you would check in with me in the next few days," Stiller continued, "sooner if there are any developments. I can start the ball rolling on a new identity, but it doesn't mean you have to agree to the relocation."

Her stomach knotted. "I suppose it makes sense to get that stuff in place."

They said their goodbyes, and Jillian clicked the disconnect button. She rested her face in her hands. Fatigue seeped into her muscles. It wasn't just the normal exhaustion from having done physical work all night.

Luke reached out and patted her arm. "I imagine this is about the time you get some sleep while the rest of the world is waking up."

She nodded. "I usually have breakfast and then go to bed." She pushed herself to her feet. "Can I fix you some eggs and sausage too?"

"Sure." He moved closer to the kitchen and sat in the chair at the table.

She pulled out a frying pan and got it sizzling before she broke eggs into it. "You're going to stay here and stand guard. Is that the plan?"

"For now. Not sure how long I can leave my deputies shorthanded. We'll figure something out."

Tonight would be her night off. Her followers would be expecting a podcast. She was going to miss them. The comments people left indicated that other insomniacs looked forward to the show. She couldn't leave them hanging. They deserved some explanation for why she had to quit the show.

When the food was ready, she set a plate down in front of Luke and then took a chair herself. The table was small and only seated two. "Mind if I say grace?"

"Not at all," said Luke.

The savory, spicy aroma swirled around her as she thanked God for the meal. She placed her napkin across her lap and dug in. She didn't realize how hungry she was, and she'd nearly finished when she said, "I agree with the marshal that I should quit the podcast..." Luke looked up and pinned her with an intense gaze, as if he knew more was coming "...but I need to do one final show."

Luke leaned back in his chair. Why was she taking so many risks? "I don't get you. The mar-

shal could set you up in a new place if you asked.
I'm sure he could move you to a temporary location even faster. Clearly the podcast has created
a problem for you, yet you can't let it go?"

"I can't abandon the loyal listeners because
of what one bad apple has done. What is a life
if you're safe, but you're not connected to other
human beings in some sort of meaningful way?"
She shifted in her seat.

He shook his head. "What is a life if you're
dead, Jillian?"

"I just think there's more to living than breathing and eating, don't you?" She rose to her feet.

"Well, sure." Had he done much besides eat
and breathe and work since Maria died? Fine,
he wasn't ever going to be romantically involved
again. But he hadn't even set any goals, taken
up a hobby or made new friends. In many ways,
he was just a man going through the motions of
being alive. Dead but still breathing.

"Meaningful connection to other human beings is important," she went on. "The people who
listen to my podcast depend on me. I'm not going
to just leave them hanging. They deserve an explanation. I'll just say that the show will be on
hiatus for personal reasons and do a final short-
ened broadcast as a way of saying goodbye."

Her comments were making him think too
much about his own life. He didn't want to argue

with her. "Why don't you get some sleep, and we'll talk about it when you wake up?"

She must be exhausted. Maybe she would see things differently once she was rested.

She nodded, slowly got up and disappeared down the hall. After he was sure she was settled, he took a short walk around the block, looking for anything suspicious. Stalkers tended to watch their prey. The patrol vehicle parked out front would go a long way toward keeping the attacker at bay.

He entered the house again making sure that the door was locked behind him. He checked out the back door, which had a view of a small field and a forest beyond. He called Deputy Walters to see if any progress had been made on finding the car the attacker had escaped in.

"That's a negative," said Angie. "I'm off shift here in just a little bit. The day-shift deputy knows to keep an eye out. You still don't know why she was attacked?"

He had to be careful in what he said. No one needed to find out that Jillian was in witness protection. The deputy would want to know why he was hanging so close to Jillian even after his shift had technically ended. "I think we're dealing with a stalker. Some other things have happened to Jillian that indicate that." He explained about the gifts and the threatening note without bringing up the podcast.

"That does sound like a stalker, very distancing and passive-aggressive. The attack at her place of work was violent though. Stalkers usually escalate gradually," said Angie.

"Yeah, it does seem inconsistent," Luke said.

They talked a few minutes more, with Luke telling her to keep looking for the vehicle—it was their only lead, after all. Then he said goodbye.

Talking to Angie and hearing her responses made him think. As he stood in Jillian's living room, it struck him that the timing of the events seemed odd. The stalker knew Jillian's work schedule. He'd attacked her knowing that the flowers with the threatening note wouldn't be found until she got off work. If his intent was to kidnap her, she wouldn't find them at all. So why leave the flowers? Had the assault at her place of work been impulsive?

He ran through the night's events in his mind and began to feel tired himself. He pulled his utility belt off and made sure his gun was within reach before lying down on the sofa.

He awoke hours later to the feeling of vibrating warmth. Marmy had settled in. The ginger cat stared at him while making biscuits on his chest. He felt heat on his legs as well. George turned out to be a large brown brindle-colored cat who had apparently overcome his shyness for the sake of warmth.

Luke drifted off to sleep again until noise outside the door caused him to wake with a start. He jerked up. George scurried away, but Marmy dug her claws into his uniform. After prying the ginger cat off his chest, he grabbed his gun and approached the door. There was no window or peephole to see who was outside.

He pressed against the door and listened, not hearing anything. After unlocking the door, he eased it open. A large empty casserole dish was resting on the porch.

He glanced around not seeing anyone, then picked up the dish. A note taped to it thanked Jillian for the meal and said it was delicious. He stepped back inside and locked the door again.

Marmy followed him into the kitchen, where he placed the casserole dish on the counter. Jillian took meals to her neighbors. It was like the woman had a compulsion to help other people. He knew she'd been a nurse in New Jersey. To avoid being tracked through their profession, people in WITSEC were discouraged to remain in the same career.

He stared out the kitchen window while the cat circled around his legs. Being around Jillian stirred him up, made him think about the condition of his own life. He wasn't sure if he liked that.

In the forest that was just on other side of the narrow field, he saw someone moving through the trees. Just a flash of bright blue against the shades of gold and red leaves, and the white of the aspen trunks.

His heart beat a little faster as he leaned closer to the window. Someone was definitely out there. Luke moved toward the door, unlocked it and hurried outside. The seconds it took to lock the door could cost him being able to catch the culprit. He ran through the field toward the aspens. The forest that bordered these houses was probably used by the residents for any number of reasons, but he had to make sure whoever was out there wasn't the man who had attacked Jillian.

When he walked deeper into the woods, the dry aspen leaves still clinging to the trees made a crackling noise as the wind blew against them. He scanned the area, but no distinctly human noises were evident. The narrow but abundant trees grew close together, not allowing him to see much of anything. He turned a slow half circle. Whoever had been here was gone.

Concerned about the door he'd left unlocked, he hurried back to the house. Once inside, he clicked the dead bolt in place and ran down the hall.

Not wanting to wake Jillian if she was still sleeping, he eased the door open and peered inside. Jillian's covers were thrown back and the bed was empty.

Quelling his rising panic, he called her name as he headed down the hall to the living room. He checked the bathroom. The house was small, so there weren't many places she could be. Marmy followed him. Her intense meowing mirrored how he felt.

The rest of the house showed no signs of a struggle. He hurried through the front door, which was also unlocked, and dashed down the porch steps.

The wind ruffled his hair as he studied the quiet street. There was a note tucked under the windshield wipers of Jillian's car on the driver's side. He pulled the piece of paper from underneath the wiper. He opened the typed note.

You are special to me. Why can't you see that?

Luke felt as if the wind had been knocked out of him. The stalker had been here, and Jillian was missing. He sped out to the sidewalk, looking up and down the street for any sign of her.

The roar of a car engine caused him to spin around. He dashed partway behind the back of his cruiser to avoid being hit as a green older model car rushed past. Adrenaline coursed through him when the driver sped up and turned a corner. He ran to driver's side door of his patrol car and got in. Then he put the vehicle in gear, backed up and zoomed down the road in the same direction the other vehicle had gone. Was Jillian in that car?

He took in a deep breath to clear out the tightness in his chest.

As he rounded the same corner the car had taken, he searched the streets, which were quiet this time of day. Everyone had gone to work, and there was no sign of the other vehicle. He drove for several blocks and checked side streets, but the car seemed to have just vanished. Was it possible the attacker lived close by and had pulled into one of the nearby garages? If this guy was mafia, he'd likely come from Jersey, but if he was a podcast stalker, he could be local.

He lifted his radio to call his deputy for backup. One thing was clear.

They needed to find Jillian. Before it was too late.

FOUR

When Jillian saw the second police car outside, she knew she'd waited too long to text Luke and let him know where she was. Her neighbor, an elderly woman named Esther, had tapped on her window, knowing that she would be sleeping. Esther's husband had fallen when he tried to stand up, and she needed help getting him back into his wheelchair. Jillian had told Esther if there was ever an emergency, she didn't mind being awakened.

At Esther's urging, Jillian had rushed through the front door, taking note that Luke was not inside. She'd assumed he'd stepped out the back door to patrol the block.

Once Esther's husband, Fred, was in his wheelchair, Jillian had taken a moment to glance out the window and observed the squad cars at her place.

Esther tugged at her lace collar from where she stood near the door. "Thank you, Jillian. I don't know what I would do without you."

Jillian glanced at Fred, who stared at the floor, and then she looked at the petite woman who took care of him 24/7. Dementia was not easy for the one receiving the care or the one giving it. "Anytime, Esther. You know that. That's what neighbors are for. Make sure that restraining belt stays around his waist so he can't try to stand."

Esther nodded. "I had it off so I could help him get into a different shirt. I just turned my back for a second."

Jillian patted Fred's shoulder. "Understandable." When Fred responded by resting his gnarled hand on hers, it sent a surge of joy through her. He could still connect with people.

"Can you stay for some cocoa and cookies?" Esther asked.

"Not today," Jillian said gently. "I have to go." After giving the older woman a pat on the shoulder, she hurried outside. Neither Luke nor the officer in the second vehicle was visible. She tried calling Luke, but there was no answer, so she sent a quick text before stepping back into the house.

Emergency with my neighbor. I'm back now.

Before she had time to take her coat off, Luke appeared at the front door. "I called my deputy. You had me scared." His voice was tinged with anger.

"I didn't mean to. I have a standing agreement

with my elderly neighbor that if I'm around, I'll come over and help her with her ailing husband."

His intense gaze gave none of his thoughts away. "Look, it's not going to work for you to stay here even if I or a deputy is on duty."

Her stomach felt like a rock had been dropped into it. "Why?"

He handed her a typed note. "This was on your windshield, and I'm pretty sure I saw someone lurking in the trees by your backyard."

The message chilled her to the marrow. The attacker knew where she worked. He knew where she lived. The threats were happening faster and faster.

"Plus, I almost got run down by a car," Luke added. "My deputy is doing a house-to-house search for the car now."

She exhaled a deep breath. "Luke, I'm sorry. Are you okay?"

He nodded. "I'm fine. He probably was watching your car and didn't like that I found the note that was meant for you."

"Was it the same car that came after me at the office and on the street when I was driving home?"

"No, but a smart criminal would have switched out cars." He picked up an empty casserole dish from the counter. "I get that people in the neighborhood depend on you, but I think you should consider going somewhere else for a bit. My family owns a farm out of town that would be pretty secure. Maybe we can set up some kind of protective detail so you can still go to work, but we'll see."

Already, the life she'd built was being ripped away from her. Soon she may have to relocate entirely. "I guess that's how it has to be."

"Think of it as a temporary measure," he said. "I know how important it is to you to stay in Spring Meadow. Give my deputies and me forty-eight hours. We'll find this guy."

His determination fortified her own resolve. "How can I help?"

"I need any details you can give me about how this guy behaves. Did you receive any other messages or gifts prior to the attack at work?"

She sat down on the couch. "There were two gifts, a stuffed animal and a bracelet, left on my front step and car in the last three days. I thought they were from a woman at church who likes to do that sort of thing, but now I don't think so."

"No notes with the previous gifts?"

She shook her head. Her mind was buzzing from the reality she was in. The cozy home she'd created was no longer safe.

"I've already sent my other deputy to check the hotels to see if anyone who raises red flags has checked in. Now we can narrow the time frame down to when the first gift showed up three days ago."

She nodded, rising to her feet and suddenly feeling overwhelmed by the whole situation. "I'm going to do that final podcast tonight. I'm set up to do it from my house. I have to stay here tonight."

"Jillian, that's not a good idea."

She stepped toward him. "Maybe one of your deputies could come by and watch outside while you're inside. The stalker might come back and then you can catch him. If he's in jail, I won't have to leave my home."

If they could take the suspect in tonight, this whole nightmare would be over for her.

Luke ran his fingers through his shaggy hair. "You're bound and determined to do that podcast, huh?"

She nodded. His mouth thinned into a tight line as he threw up his hands.

"I'm glad we have an understanding," she said.

"Is that what we have?" He let out a heavy breath. "I don't understand you at all."

She picked up on the note of frustration in his voice. But she wouldn't budge. If she needed to leave eventually, fine, but she'd say goodbye to her listeners and give herself time to leave the home she'd made. "I'm not going to go back to sleep. My normal routine is to clean my house, have dinner, and then toward nightfall, I do the podcast."

"If we're going to insist on spending a few more hours here, maybe setting a trap for this guy will work. Once Deputy Tyler is done canvassing the neighborhood, he can stand watch outside while I'm in here with you. I'll have him switch out his patrol car for a civilian car. And it would be good if I could hide my patrol vehicle. If the attacker knows there's a police presence, he won't move in."

"You should be able to fit it in my garage," she said.

Jillian tidied her house, changed out the cat boxes and fixed dinner for herself and Luke. The sky had grown dark by the time the deputy returned in plain clothes and an unmarked car. In September, it got dark a little after dinner time.

Luke advised the deputy to focus on watching the trees behind Jillian's house. "I can stay inside and keep an eye on the street out front. Check in with me at least every fifteen minutes."

Deputy Tyler nodded and headed outside.

From where she stood near the door, Jillian took a deep breath as tension threaded through her body. "I guess this is it." Marmy followed her down the hall as she stepped into her bedroom. She saw that George had taken up his position underneath the covers again. At least one of them was relaxed, she thought as she drew back the curtain on her closet/studio, then sat down to do her final podcast for *Voice in the Night*.

As she opened up the laptops, she heard Luke approach, and he peered over her shoulder. "Do people leave comments about the show when it's going on."

"Yes. Here, I'll show you." She clicked on the keyboard. "One laptop is to read the comments as they come in, and the other will show that my levels are okay, so my voice is modulated."

Luke leaned over even more to get closer to the laptop. He was so close that she could smell that woodsy scent of his cologne again. His proximity made her heart beat a little faster.

She cleared her throat. "Maybe you should grab a chair." She pointed to one in the corner of the room.

"Sorry." He walked across the floor and returned, scooting the chair over to the laptop. "Have you ever gotten a comment that seemed inappropriate?"

"Nothing that sent up a red flag. What kind of things would you look for?"

"Something that might presume some sort of closeness between the two of you or an overreaction or misinterpretation of something you said on the air."

Jillian tried to think. She'd done the podcast for

almost three years and didn't recall anything like that. Yet what Luke said set her on edge. Would the stalker be listening tonight? "I have to start in less than two minutes."

Luke nodded. "I'm going to be checking these comments as they come in."

Her attention was on the computer clock as she spoke. "The show is archived on a couple of platforms. I may not have seen all the comments that came in after the show aired, but maybe we could find them."

She watched the countdown and pulled the microphone closer to her face. "Good evening," she began. "This is your resident insomniac, and I am the Voice in the Night. Tonight's broadcast will be a short one…"

She plowed ahead, giving her listeners a brief explanation that tonight would be her final show. She left Luke to monitor the comments as she continued the broadcast, reading Scripture, offering encouragement and playing worship songs for another fifteen minutes.

"We're getting close to having to say goodbye. Here is one of my favorite hymns." She muted her mic as the song began to play. She sat up in her chair and took a breath, removing her headphones.

"I need to check in with my deputy," Luke whispered, softly scooting his chair back. He stood up and left the room. She could hear him talking on his radio as she did her final sign-off. A sadness settled around her after.

Luke stood in the doorway. "My deputy isn't responding when I radio him. I need to go check to see if he's all right. Lock the door behind me."

Her heart beat a little faster. "Okay."

As he turned and headed down the hallway, she pushed her chair back and stared at her broadcast equipment for a long moment before moving toward the doorway. After hurrying down the hall, she stepped into the kitchen…and noticed the back door was open. Had Luke done that? She had a feeling he wouldn't, but maybe in his haste… She was a few feet from the door when the kitchen went black.

The lights in the living room had gone off as well.

The electricity was out. No moonlight shone through the windows. She fumbled for the lock on the door, clicking it into place. Then she stepped toward the living room where, she kept a flashlight in one of the side table drawers.

She groaned when she bumped into the vacuum that she'd left out.

Another noise reached her ears. It sounded almost like a gust of wind, but it had come from inside the house.

Jillian's heart pounded against her rib cage. The house had grown silent again. Where had the noise come from? Moving carefully, she reached for the drawer where she kept the flashlight. She eased it open and felt for the flashlight, pulling it out but not turning it on.

A creaking noise reached her ears.

"Who's there?"

Before she had a chance to turn on the flashlight, a weight landed on her body. Someone grappled her to the floor, and she screamed as she fell back, twisting to get free. She could hear heavy breathing as the man wrapped an iron grip on her throat.

Using the flashlight as a weapon, she struck him several times as she struggled for breath. He released the hold he had on her neck but slammed her head against the floor.

She had the sensation of floating, and then everything went black.

When she came to. The house was quiet. Had she lost consciousness for only a few seconds or longer? She didn't know.

Then she heard the creek of a floorboard. Someone was still in the house. He seemed to be rummaging around for something, but she didn't know what. Did he mean to tie her up? She didn't want to find out.

She had to get out of here. She rushed toward the back door, turned the lock and flung it open. Then she ran into the darkness.

* * *

Luke's heart shifted into overdrive when he found his deputy lying on the ground a few feet inside the aspen forest.

He knelt and shook the man's shoulder. "Hey, Chris."

The deputy groaned. "Got knocked on the head." His voice was weak.

Luke took in a breath. This was sabotage. "Can you get up?"

"Yes." Despite his positive response, Deputy Tyler still sounded a bit detached.

"We've got to go. Jillian might be in danger." Luke didn't wait to see if his deputy got back on his feet. Chris could take care of himself. And Luke had a feeling the attacker wouldn't be after Chris again—only Jillian. He probably just wanted to make sure Chris couldn't interfere with getting at Jillian.

Emerging from the trees, Luke saw that the house had gone dark. He drew his weapon and kept running. Nearly at the door, Jillian collided with him, falling into his arms.

"Someone's in there," she said raggedly. "He must have thrown the breaker switch in the garage."

"Stay close to me." Luke pulled his flashlight off his utility belt and entered the dark house. He arced his light but didn't see anything in the kitchen or the living room. He moved toward the door that connected with the attached garage, speaking in a whisper to Jillian. "Stay back. Get down."

He unlocked the door, kicked it open and prepared for gunfire. His light revealed only his patrol vehicle and storage shelves.

Jillian's frantic voice reached his ears. "I hear noise in the bedroom."

He turned, hurried down the hall and encountered a shut door. Crashing sounds emanated from the bedroom. He kicked open the door just in time to see a dark figure crawling through the window.

Luke followed after him, climbing out the window. When he hit the sidewalk, he pressed the button on his radio as he ran toward the sound of retreating footsteps. "Chris, I need your help. Suspect is on the move up Elm Street, headed toward the park."

Chris's reply came immediately. "On it." His deputy's voice sounded stronger than it had moments ago.

Still holding the flashlight in one hand and his gun in the other, Luke sprinted in the direction the attacker had gone. In his peripheral vision, he saw Deputy Tyler run toward him at a diagonal.

Both men entered the park. Wind blew against the swings on the playground, causing the chains to make squeaking noises. Deputy Tyler moved deeper into the park while Luke ran around the perimeter, scanning the forest that bordered it. He could see the other officer's flashlight beam by the swings. Other than that, he saw no moving shadows, and he didn't hear any footsteps. The culprit could be hiding, but he doubted it was in the park, which wasn't that big.

The deputy's voice came across the radio. "Nothing here."

"Why don't you search the forest?" Luke said. "I need to get back and make sure Jillian is safe." He worried that the attacker might double-back and go after Jillian when she was vulnerable. He'd already let that happen once when he'd been lured out of the house looking for Chris, which might have been part of the attacker's plan.

"Ten-four," said Deputy Tyler.

Luke jogged back to the house. The front door was locked, but he found the back door open. He stepped inside the dark house. "Jillian?"

Her voice floated up the hallway from the bedroom.

"In here." She sounded upset.

Well, she had every right to be. And they couldn't stay here. He needed to get her to the farm as soon as possible. His mom would be out of town for a few days. His brother and his family lived on the property but far enough away that they wouldn't be in harm's way. He'd let them know that Jillian was staying at the house because someone had attacked her and might again if she was found. He didn't need to give away much else.

He stepped into the garage and threw the breaker. Through the open door of the garage, he watched the lights in the living room come on. He stepped back into the house and hurried down the hallway.

He entered the bedroom, where Jillian stood by the table with the recording equipment. One of the laptops had been knocked to the floor. She held the other laptop in her hand.

"He…he left me another message." Her voice faltered.

Tension threaded around his torso as Luke stepped toward her. She turned the laptop so he could see it.

How dare you quit the broadcast. You will pay.

The attempt to set a trap for the stalker hadn't worked. Jillian couldn't stay here any longer. The threat against her life was all too real.

FIVE

"Jillian, did you hear what I said?"

As she sat in the passenger seat of Luke's patrol vehicle, Jillian couldn't stop her racing thoughts. "I'm sorry. Were you talking?"

Luke turned down a country road and drove over a bridge. His farm was at least half an hour outside of town.

She stared out at the night as stars twinkled in the cloudless sky. Now that the attacker had been bold enough to break into her house, it was clear she couldn't stay at her home. She'd packed up a few things and put the cats in their carriers. She brought her cleaning supplies with her. Luke had suggested that she might still be able to go to work if she had protection.

"Given what has happened, the way this guy is escalating to breaking into your home and attacking you anytime you go out in public, I feel I need to be with you. You can hide out at the farm for a few days and while my deputies and

I catch this guy. You're not to contact anyone in the meantime…and you should take a few days off work."

Though she'd been hopeful about still being able to work, she knew he was right. "I hope this doesn't last long. How is it going to look that I'm not at my house? I suddenly up and leave with no explanation to my neighbors…people might wonder about that." The town was small enough that people talked, and the gossip channels were turned on a high volume. She wondered, too, how Esther would do with Fred if she wasn't there.

"Just say that you needed a break and wanted to get out of town."

She wasn't totally on board about the deception, but what choice did she have? At least at Luke's farm, she'd be near home…and maybe in a few days she could return to work. She'd lost her home and her podcast in one night. She didn't want to lose more of what she had managed to establish in this town. Though she knew her boss, Eloise, would be understanding, she couldn't afford to take too many days off.

They drove past a fenced field with cows in it. Up ahead, she saw a two-story house surrounded by barns and outbuildings. Light glowed in one of the downstairs windows of the main house.

They passed a hand-painted sign that said *U pick pumpkins and squash.*

"People come out here for their fall vegetables?" she asked.

"Yes." Luke pulled up to the farmhouse beside an older-looking truck. "We grow strawberries in the summer for people to pick. Ever since my dad died, we've been selling off acreage. The u-pick stuff is a way for the remaining land to bring in some money. It doesn't make enough to support any of us just to cover expenses and upkeep. Both my brother and I have jobs in town. Mom has a quilting business, as well."

She nodded. "Has the land been in the family long?"

"Four generations." A note of sadness colored his words. His voice seemed to intensify when he talked about the farm.

He pushed open the car door. "Come on, I'll help you get settled."

Luke rounded the car and grabbed her suitcase from the trunk while she picked up both the cat carriers from the back seat. He walked in front of her up the porch stairs and pushed open the door. "It's usually unlocked, but you can keep it locked while you're here."

She glanced back toward the fields of crops and the u-pick stand, which was some distance from the house.

She stepped into a large living room with leather furniture and a cowhide rug. A large kitchen was visible on the other side of the space. This whole thing, being a stranger in someone else's home, felt a little uncomfortable. Hopefully, it would just be a few days and she could get back to her old life.

"Why don't you let the cats out? Have them get used to their new digs. Mom has an old cat, so there's a box already. He pretty much stays in her sewing room so there shouldn't be any trouble between the cats."

"I'll put out their box too. It's still in your car." She unzipped the cat carriers. Marmy jumped out and began poking around. George remained in the carrier.

"Here, I'll show you your room."

"I think I'll take George with me." She lifted the carrier after zipping it shut. The cat yowled as she followed Luke up the stairs.

He moved down a hallway and pointed at one of the doors. "Mom isn't here right now because she's at a quilting show. She'll be gone a few days." He pointed to another door. "That's my room." He stopped at the next door and pushed it open. "This is the guest room."

Still holding George in his carrier, she stepped into a room that had a very pioneer feel to it. A quilt done in purples and blues decorated the bed. The room was filled with antique furniture. Only the landscape photos on the wall looked modern.

"I'll let you get settled. I have to go feed the barn animals, but I'll be right back."

She put the carrier down on the bed and opened it. George still wouldn't jump out. "I'll go with you. I don't sleep at night, remember?" She found herself not wanting to be alone in the house.

"Suit yourself," he said.

The chill of the September night sank into her skin as they walked out of the house and up a path that led to a barn, where a brown horse with a strip of white on its nose was in one of the stalls.

The horse whinnied and raised its head when Luke stepped inside. He walked over to her. "Hey, old girl." Luke stroked the horse's muzzle before turning slightly toward Jillian. "This is Princess. She's been my horse since I was a teenager. You want to say hi to her?"

"Sure." Jillian stepped toward the stall.

Luke lifted her hand toward the horse. "She likes to be scratched behind the ears."

Her small hand fit so well into his large calloused one. The surge of warmth she felt at his touch surprised her. The horse lowered its head when she reached toward the ears.

Luke spoke in soothing tones while he scratched behind the horse's other ear. "She's the only livestock of mine left. The other farm animals are boarders who bring in some money."

Luke moved toward a different part of the barn and returned with a bucket full of food. He opened up the stall and set the bucket down. After leading the horse out to eat, he and Jillian cleaned out the stall and put fresh hay in it for the horse. He gave gentle and encouraging instructions as she helped out, and she found working with him to be relaxing, even fun.

Luke led Jillian through the darkness to another barn, where two alpacas and a pig were in need of food. "So, you do all of this at the end of a long workday."

"I'm the one who wanted to board animals. So, yes, it's kind of my responsibility. My niece, my brother's kid, brings the animals in from the field earlier in the day." Luke pointed off in the distance. "You can't see the house from here cause it's over the hill, but my brother and his wife live over there. Matt moved the modular home onto the property once he got married."

Luke had to be Jillian's age or a little older, yet he was single. She knew it wasn't her business, but she found herself asking, "You never wanted to build your own place to…marry and have kids?"

Silence hung between them for a moment. "Just didn't work out that way for me," he said.

His words had taken on a dark tone. There was probably more to that story. She didn't say anything, hoping to give him more room to share. After all, he no doubt knew how she'd lost her fiancé. They walked on, the sound of their feet hitting the packed dirt the only noise in the still of the night.

Luke sighed. "After Dad died, Matt was put in charge of the farm. He's the oldest, so that's how it goes."

The tone of his voice changed yet again. What was that she heard in his words, a note of frustration or bitterness? His mind had traveled from whatever reason he had for not getting married to the arrangement for how the farm was run. It was clear he was not a man who wore his heart on his sleeve. Luke was far more complicated than she'd initially thought.

He said nothing further and they returned to the house. Luke showed her where some things were in the kitchen and then excused himself. "If you don't mind, I have to get up early for work. I'd like to get a few hours' sleep."

"Sure, no problem." She stepped toward him, grabbing his sleeve. "Thanks for giving me a place to stay."

He met her gaze. "It's the least I can do. I'm charged with watching over you."

When she looked at him this closely, his eyes appeared more gray than brown in this light. "I appreciate it all the same."

Marmy wandered into the kitchen and meowed up at Jillian. She knelt to gather the cat into her arms.

"I'm sorry about you having to call off work. It's just safer if you stay here hidden away." He stepped toward the threshold of the kitchen. "Hopefully, we'll get this guy in custody soon. My deputies and I will make it a priority."

She'd have to call her boss in the morning.

She listened to the sound of him going up the stairs. Jillian did not feel at all tired. She made herself a cup of tea and a snack while Marmy swirled around her legs. After she finished her tea, she wandered through the downstairs with the ginger cat following her. She peeked through the open door of a corner room behind the stairs that was filled with fabric, sewing machines and a quilting long arm. This must be where Luke's mother worked.

The old cat that Luke had mentioned, a gray fellow with a white tuft of hair on his chest, rested on a chair. The cat only lifted its head slightly in reaction to seeing Marmy.

"Are you two going to try to be friends?"

Jillian smiled at the felines, then traipsed upstairs to her room. As she moved past Luke's closed door, she heard no sound. He must already be asleep.

When she entered her room, she took note of

the lump in the quilt. George had found his safe spot. She pulled a book from her suitcase and sat down in the chair by the window, staring out at the night sky and the half moon.

When she took her phone out of a coat pocket, she noticed that she had a text. It wasn't a number that was in her contacts. She clicked on the message.

Where did you go, sweet Jillian?

The message sent chills through her. The attacker didn't know where she was hiding out, but he'd still found a way to remind her he was out there. She checked the phone number the text had come from. It was different from the call that had been made to her while she was at work. The stalker might be using a burner phone so he couldn't be tracked. She'd have to tell Luke about it in the morning. He needed to get his sleep.

She rose from the chair and paced the floor before grabbing a throw off the end of the bed and wrapping it around her shoulders. She sat back down in the chair and drew the blanket close to her neck for comfort.

Jillian opened her book and prepared for the long sleepless night ahead, but when she tried to read, the words on the page blurred. She placed her hand on her chest where her heart was still pounding. She could not get the creepy text out of her mind.

* * *

Luke had just filled his thermos with coffee in the kitchen, where morning sun shone through the window, when his phone rang. Deputy Angie Walters.

"Good morning. Whatcha got for me, Angie?"

"I asked around the hotels to see if anyone who gave off a bad vibe had checked in since Jillian received that first gift. Got a couple of names for you, and one of them has a record, name of Stanley Reese."

"Good work. Can you pull a photo of the guy and send it to me?"

"I can do that. Should we question Stanley?"

"No, I don't want him to know we're onto him."

"I can tail him until I get another call," Angie offered. "We can put someone else on the other guy, as well. His name is Jon Wilson."

"Sounds good but focus on the guy with the record. I don't know if Chris told you or not, but Jillian is staying with me out at the farm. She's just too vulnerable at her home. He broke into her house."

"I read through Chris's report to get up to speed."

Angie was always on top of everything. He appreciated what a good deputy she was. "I'll see you in a bit." He set his phone down and, sensing that someone had stepped into the room, he turned.

Jillian stood on the threshold holding her cell.

"I thought you'd be sleeping," he said.

"I caught a few hours. I hope you got rested up."

"Roaring and ready to go." He lifted his thermos.

She held the phone out to him. "He contacted me last night." Her voice had an icy tone to it.

He took her cell and read the text. The content made it clear why she would be upset. Calling her "sweet Jillian" implied a delusional connection. "So, he doesn't know that you're here. That's one good thing."

She shrugged. "For now, he doesn't know. He's good at finding things out about me."

He nodded. She had a point, but he wouldn't let that happen. "Look, I got to go into work. I'll be back tonight. You'll be safe here, and I'll check in with you when I can. The best way I can help you is to put this guy in a jail cell. I told my brother and mom that you needed to stay here but kept the details vague. They won't talk. Do you think you can get some more sleep?"

"I'll try."

"You're safe here, Jillian," he said again. "My sister-in-law, Tasha, will be manning the u-pick booth. It's open limited hours and it's not close to the house. All you've got to do is stay inside and out of view."

"Like a prisoner," she said.

He reached out to brush his hand over her arm. "This whole thing is very temporary."

"I hope so. Do you think I should take Marshal Stiller up on his offer?" Her voice was filled with anguish.

"I've lived in Spring Meadow my whole life. I can't imagine what it would be like to have to walk away from everything I know and then to have to do it twice."

She tilted her head as her eyes glazed over. She leaned toward him. "This is so hard," she said.

"I know." Her being so close made his heart beat faster. She was clearly in deep pain. He wanted so badly to hold her and tell her everything would be okay, but it wasn't his place. She was only here so he could protect her, and he needed to keep his distance.

She stepped away and cleared her throat. "Thank you for letting me stay in your home."

He handed her phone back to her. Her fingers brushed over his when she took it.

"Oh, I almost forgot," she continued. "The phone number this text came from and the call while I was at work came from two different numbers."

"Might be he's using a burner phone and discarding it, but we can look into it. Send me the numbers." He reached out without thinking and patted her arm just above the elbow. "The house will be nice and quiet for you today."

She nodded. "The cats and I will be fine." He heard hesitation in her voice.

He headed toward the front door and out to his patrol vehicle. He waved to Tasha and her two daughters as they set up the u-pick stand.

He drove out on the dirt road back toward town. A small van came toward him. He veered off toward the shoulder on the narrow road, catching a glimpse of the hunched down man behind the wheel as he went by. The only place he could be going would be the farm to buy vegetables. There was only one other resident on this road, and he didn't get much company.

Tightness wove through his chest.

He debated if he should turn the car around and go back. He watched as the van turned into the farm and then took the road that led to the u-pick stand. He continued to watch as the man got out and approached Tasha. At no time did the man glance toward the house.

His radio crackled, and he picked it up. Dispatch came on the line. "Two-car collision. Just west of town on I-90. Highway patrol is asking for an assist."

He glanced over his shoulder where the trees

that lined the farm were visible. "Can Angie or another deputy take it?"

"Angie is out on a shoplifting call. One of the drivers is belligerent. May have had a little too much of the happy sauce."

He smiled at the dispatcher's colorful choice of words. Mary Ellen was his mother's age and had been a dispatcher since before he'd come on the force.

He had to do his job. He pulled out on the road and headed toward town but not before calling Jillian to remind her to stay out of sight. The u-pick stand was some distance from the main house, but he didn't want to take any chances.

His mind kept going back to thoughts of Jillian. He was drawn to her and he couldn't say why. Maybe it was just his need to protect her. As he got to the outskirts of town, he prayed that Jillian would be safe.

SIX

Standing off to the side, Jillian watched from an upstairs window as Tasha and her two dark-haired daughters, who looked to be under the age of six, directed customers to where they could harvest squash, corn and other fall vegetables. She narrowed her eyes to make out more details. A stretch of road and field stood between the main house and where the vegetables were sold.

Jillian had gotten herself some breakfast and then slept for a few hours. When she woke up, she had a text from Marshal Stiller asking for a status report.

She got him up to date on the move out to Luke's farm and then she called her boss to let her know she couldn't come into work for personal reasons.

Eloise was understanding.

The remainder of the day would be taken up hiding inside while life went on for the rest of the world. From an upstairs window, she had a view of most of the farm.

One of the customers, a man wearing a baseball hat, glanced up at the window where she was standing. Heart pounding, she stepped back into the shadows. She thought she'd been out of view. From now on, she wasn't even going to look out a window no matter how bored she was.

Noises downstairs caused her to take in a jagged breath. Had she remembered to lock the downstairs door after Luke left? She heard footsteps and then a woman's singsong voice. "Hello? Jillian?"

She let out a gust of air, releasing the tightness that had embedded in her chest. Luke's mom? She hurried down the stairs with Marmy following her.

A tall woman holding several quilts with a set of keys dangling from her fingers stood in the open doorway. A streak of purple ran through the woman's dark hair, which was pulled up into a loose bun. Her gaze traveled upward as a smile graced her face. "You must be Jillian."

The warmth the woman radiated drew her in. "Yes, Luke said he got you up to speed. I didn't realize you were going to be back so soon." Luke had implied that she would be here alone.

"I finished early. So sorry to hear about someone attacking you like that." She tilted her head toward Marmy who was swirling around Jillian's legs. "And he told me about the cats."

She reached toward the quilts. "Can I help you, Mrs. Mayfair?"

"Please call me Charlotte." She placed the quilts in Jillian's open arms. "You can take those to my workroom. I'll run outside and get the rest of my stuff."

Charlotte pivoted and moved toward the open door back out to her car.

She'd have to remember to lock the door once Charlotte was back inside. Jillian moved down the hall to the corner room where Luke's mom had her quilting studio. She set the quilts down on a wide table. The old cat she'd seen last night was still in the same chair. Fabric in every color and print design imaginable was folded and stacked in a wall of shelves. Several incomplete quilts hung on the opposite wall.

Charlotte entered, carrying more quilts and a case with a handle. The older woman set the quilts down and opened up another storage area that held completed quilts. Charlotte then put the quilts away. "These are the ones that didn't sell. Talked to a lot of people. Had some interest in the classes I teach."

Jillian continued to admire the colors and patterns of fabric.

Charlotte closed the doors where her pieces

were stored and turned to face Jillian. "I know what you're thinking. This many sewing supplies is overkill, but you know what they say. She who dies with the most fabric and incomplete projects wins."

Jillian laughed. "Actually, I was just thinking how beautiful all the fabric is."

"Careful. That is the first step to becoming a quilting addict."

Jillian laughed again. "I'm not doing anything right now. Can I help you with something in here?"

"Luke thought you might need to sleep during the day because you are in the habit of working at night."

She shrugged. "I slept some, but right now I'm wide awake."

"Well then, I'll put you to work," said Charlotte.

Jillian was grateful to have something to do besides read the book she'd brought with her to pass the time. Charlotte pulled some fabric from her stash. "I need me some five-inch squares of fabric. We're going to make some HSTs, half-square triangles."

Charlotte showed Jillian how to measure the squares. The two women worked side by side. Jillian was grateful for the company and for something to do.

"You must love doing this," said Jillian.

"I do. Wish I could do more of it. There's a lot of other work connected with the farm that feels like a distraction to me since my husband died. Making sure the plants are watered, weeded and fertilized. Tasha and I take turns running the stand. Luke and Matt handle keeping the equipment going."

"You don't like living out here?"

"Used to love it when my husband was alive. We worked together on things. I've had some health scares in the last year. What I'd really like to do is to sell this place and use my share to open a quilt shop in town, maybe with a little apartment above it. Teach my classes from there. I'd probably get a lot more interest. It's a bit of a drive to get out here, especially in the winter. And traveling to places to do the classes wears on me."

"Luke likes the farm," Jillian said.

"He always did more so than his brother. Back when he was engaged to Maria, the plan was for him to take over the farm. Matt wanted to get his business degree and move away."

Jillian tensed at that. She hadn't realized... "Luke was engaged?"

"He didn't tell you." Charlotte handed Jillian another piece of fabric. "Doesn't surprise me. He never was big on sharing about himself. She died in a single-car crash on the way back from a wedding dress fitting."

"That's tragic." Jillian set the fabric scrap she'd been holding down on the worktable and stared at the floral pattern as her thoughts raced. Luke had experienced a total upheaval in his life just like she had. Her heart ached for him. They had more in common than she'd realized.

"Probably should have kept my mouth shut," Charlotte said. "Don't tell him I said anything. He's a very private person." She grabbed fabric from her pile, unfolded it and smoothed it with her hands.

"I won't say anything," Jillian replied.

"I try to respect his wishes. But I'm his mom. I can't help but worry." Charlotte placed the larger piece of fabric on the ironing board. Steam rose up when she pressed it. "I just think if he opened up a little more, he'd be able to move on with his life."

The fabric was still warm when Charlotte handed it to Jillian to cut. While Jillian cut the squares, Charlotte pieced them together and sewed them. Jillian's mind was still on what Charlotte had shared about Luke.

Jillian helped Charlotte pin the completed HSTs on the part of the wall that had a sort of soft bulletin board. They stood back to look at the squares.

"HSTs are pretty versatile." Charlotte elbowed Jillian. "Go ahead and put a design together."

"Really?" Feeling a little intimidated, Jillian stared at the different colors and patterns and slowly rearranged them on the wall.

They stood back to look at what she had come up with.

Charlotte patted Jillian's shoulder. "You have good instincts."

Jillian shrugged. "I just put them together in a way that made me happy."

"That's the best way to do it."

"I'm sure there are rules about the best way to piece the fabric," said Jillian.

"Ah, yes, the rules are rather a moving target depending on who you talk to," Charlotte replied.

Jillian helped her work a bit longer before she started to yawn. "Guess I'm feeling sleepy again."

Charlotte set her work down. "Why don't I fix you an early dinner or late lunch, whatever you want to call it? I'm sure you'd like to try to rest."

Charlotte's warmth and hospitality was like a soothing balm. The two women ate together, and then Jillian excused herself to go upstairs. She fell asleep with Marmy nestled against her back and George purring close to her head.

As she drifted off, she noted how comfortable she'd become in the farmhouse since first arriving last night. And she prayed that whoever was after her would never find her here.

The sound of her phone ringing woke her up. Fear sliced through her until she looked at the number. Her boss. Until this guy was caught, every phone call and text would make her tense up. She clicked the connect button as she sat up.

"Hello, Eloise."

"Jillian I am so sorry to bother you."

She picked up on the tone of desperation in her boss's voice and rose to her feet. She'd slept a long time. It was dark outside. "What's up?"

"I know you said you needed a couple of days off."

"Yes." Jillian had a feeling she knew where this was going.

"One of my girls quit half an hour before her shift was going to start. I was going to have Adele take your building tonight, but she just called in sick." Her voice increased in intensity and speed. "I can cover for my gal that quit."

Jillian's stomach knotted up. Eloise was a widow in her late sixties and not in good health. Cleaning an office building would be hard for her let alone two. As the manager, Eloise's job was to supervise, train and schedule but anytime they were shorthanded, Eloise had to pick up the slack.

Downstairs she heard the sound of Luke coming in the house.

"Can you give me ten minutes? I'll get back to you." Jillian had not given Eloise the details of why she needed time off. She was worried too about the loss of income from not working.

"Sure. Thank you, Jillian. I appreciate you. You're my best employee."

With her phone still in her hand, Jillian hurried downstairs to talk to Luke. She may be leaving the farm sooner than expected.

The weariness of a long day weighed on Luke's shoulders as he watched Jillian come down the stairs.

"Any progress on catching the man who came after me?" she asked.

He saw that look of hope in her eyes. He hated letting her down. "Nothing yet. We're looking into a couple out of town guys who arrived about the time those gifts showed up. One guy Stanley Reese has a record. The other guy is named Jon Wilson. Nothing suspicious about him but it's not clear why he's in town."

"Jon Wilson sounds like a made-up name."

"Yeah, I guess. Jillian what's going on?"

She pressed the phone against her shoulder. "Luke, I know you said I need to lay low and take time off work."

"Something's happened?"

"My boss just called. She's short-handed. That's

why I was hoping you had caught the guy. Eloise could lose her cleaning contract if the work doesn't get done. She does this job to supplement her social security."

"No," said Luke. "You can't go to that office building alone." Even before he finished the sentence, the big wide eyes told him what she had in mind.

"I know it's asking a lot. But I'm worried about Eloise."

Hadn't he learned before that arguing with her was futile? "Okay," said Luke after a long moment. "I'll go with you."

She jumped the short distance between them and wrapped her arms around him. "Thank you."

Even though she backed off quickly, the hug made his heart beat a little faster.

Within fifteen minutes she was ready to leave. Luke drove, staring through the windshield of his truck at the darkness and the tree-lined country road with his mind still on Jillian's safety. He'd brought his personal firearm with him and called the deputy on duty to do a patrol by the building.

Jillian's voice interrupted his thoughts.

"I really appreciate this. It helps Eloise and I'm a little worried about money if I take too much time off." Her work caddy sat between them in the cab of the truck. He'd helped her load the vacuum into the truck bed.

Jillian had seemed different toward him since he got home. He couldn't quite pinpoint it. There was a softness in her voice, and her gaze seemed to linger on him. He wondered why. He also wondered why his mom kept saying what a "nice girl" Jillian was while he'd eaten a quick dinner and Jillian gathered her cleaning supplies.

He was concerned about his mom being back sooner than expected. Maybe he could talk her into leaving.

"It's important to help people if we can, right?" She was an inspiration to him in that way. Until Jillian came into his life, he hadn't realized how shut down he'd been. Not how a Christian should live.

"I know this is a lot of extra work for you," she said.

"It's my job."

"No, I would say it was above and beyond your job. Don't you need some downtime?" She seemed awful interested in talking about his life.

"Any free time I have is taken up by the farm." The land stretched him thin most days, yet he couldn't imagine his life without it.

The lights of the city came into view. "There's a coffee hut I always stop at on my way to work," Jillian murmured.

"I've gone there before a stakeout or night

shift. You're talking about the one that is open twenty-four hours. What's it called?"

"The Coffee Experience. What a name, huh?"

"Guess all the good ones were taken."

They both laughed.

Luke drove past a few scattered houses and a farm equipment business before pulling up to the coffee place. An outdoor light illuminated the hut, and a warm glow emanated from within.

Luke rolled down his window, allowing the cool autumn breeze in.

A thin man wearing glasses stuck his head out the drive-through window. "Hey, Sheriff Mayfair."

Jillian leaned forward so she was visible. "Hey, Roger."

The man's expression changed, his eyes growing wide with surprise. "Jillian?" His eyes bounced between her and Luke. "Is everything okay?"

They'd known this might happen—that people might see them around town together late at night and wonder about it. He preferred that the locals didn't come to any conclusions about Jillian being in protective custody. While she was still in witness protection, he didn't want to draw any undue attention to her.

"Luke is just taking me to work while my car is out of commission." Jillian leaned toward Luke and rested her hand on his arm. "Isn't he thought-ful?"

The gesture was meant to be part of the ruse they'd discussed before leaving the house, that they were a couple. Yet her nearness, the scent of her floral perfume whirling around him, made his heart flutter.

"Oh, sure." Roger looked off to the side as his voice took on a lower tone. "Didn't know you two were together…"

Jillian beamed up at him like someone fresh in love. "It's new…" She glanced at Luke warmly. "We've been taking it slow."

He held her gaze a moment, his throat tighten-ing before he glanced away.

Roger nodded slowly, then smiled. "The usual for you, Jillian?"

"Yes, I don't have my cup with me."

"I'll just have an Americano. Thanks," said Luke.

"Sure, Sheriff." Roger closed the drive-through window to prepare the drinks.

"You and Roger seem pretty friendly," Luke observed. He noticed how the man's voice dropped when he learned Luke and Jillian were an item.

"I see him six nights a week. I know lots of night people. Sometimes I go to that café that's open all night on the edge of town when I can't sleep. It's almost always the same crowd. The doctors and nurses getting off shift. The artist and the older woman who works the night shift at the convenience store, people who just got off the bus."

"Night people?" Luke said. "I never thought of it that way. If I pull graveyard patrol, I'm ready to sleep when I get home."

Roger handed the prepared drinks through the window. Luke placed his in the cupholder.

"I got this." Jillian handed Luke a bill to give to Roger. "Keep the change."

"Thanks, Jillian." Roger looked past Luke to make eye contact with Jillian. "Us night people need to stick together, right?"

"For sure." She lifted her cup to him.

He placed the bill in the cash register and slammed the drawer. "You two have a good night." His eyes narrowed as he waved them off before closing the window. He was clearly disappointed that Jillian was taken. Was it an innocent crush, or was his interest in Jillian more sinister?

Luke drove to the office building and parked close to the entrance. "I'll follow you in. Make sure the place is clear."

"Do you think he'll come back here?" Jillian pushed open the door and lifted her caddy.

"Hard to say. I've got one deputy on duty tonight. Angus Smith is older and semi-retired.

While you were getting your stuff together, I called him and asked him to do a drive-by and hang close. He'll be able to do that as long as he doesn't have to deal with another call."

Jillian nodded. "There's part of me that hopes he comes back tonight so you can catch him."

Luke had thought of that too. Maybe that had been part of her motivation in wanting to go back to the office. Though he wasn't totally on board with Jillian being bait.

The wind ruffled Luke's hair as he pulled the vacuum out of the truck bed. A few trees bordered the building, and the land around the parking lot sloped downward. There was only one entrance into the parking lot and only a scant amount of vegetation for someone to hide behind.

He took note of the four-digit code as Jillian punched it in.

"Is that often changed?"

"Only once in the three years that I've been working here."

Spring Meadow wasn't a high-crime city. People tended to get lax about security. He glanced around again. Could someone have watched from a distance with binoculars and figured out the code or had a way to bypass it?

She tilted her head toward him. "I make it a habit to stand in front of the panel, so the keypad isn't visible."

She seemed to know what he was thinking.

Jillian pushed open the door. "I know this guy who is after me is probably the worst thing you've had to deal with in a long time, but because of what went down in Jersey, I just got in the habit of taking precautions."

She stepped across the entrance, holding the door open for him. Her comment jarred him into alertness. The reality that Jillian lived with was that she would always be looking over her shoulder, even after this attacker was caught.

Once inside, Luke pulled his weapon and did a quick search of the ground floor. They walked over to the elevator together. He got on, carrying the vacuum after she was inside. The doors slid shut and she pushed the number three.

The elevator hummed and then stopped suddenly. No floor number came up on the LED panel.

After giving Luke a nervous glance, Jillian reached toward the panel and pushed the number three again.

The elevator didn't move.

Pushing the emergency button would do no good, since there was no one else in the building. He pulled his phone out to call his deputy.

The elevator started up again. He let out the breath he'd been holding. "Probably just some kind of glitch."

The doors opened up, and they both stepped out into a dark hallway. He heard Jillian's hand swish against the wall and click the light switch. No lights came on.

"Something's wrong," she said.

Light flashed several feet from him as a dark mass came toward him. A hard object collided with the side of his head.

He reached out for the support of a wall even as his knees buckled.

The last thing he heard was Jillian screaming.

SEVEN

In the flash of light, Jillian saw the man dressed in black hit Luke. The space was dark, but she could hear him crumple to the floor.

Her breathing became rapid and shallow as she pressed against the wall and moved to get away from the assailant.

A hand reached out and grabbed her sleeve. She yanked herself free and took off running.

Behind her she could hear Luke moaning. He'd only lost consciousness for a moment.

Gunfire erupted from behind her, and the sound echoed in the quiet building. Her whole body jerked. She prayed that Luke had not been hit. The muzzle blast told her where the assailant was.

She dropped down on her hands and knees and crawled toward one of the outer office carrels. She scrunched herself into a corner and listened as the assailant stalked around. Her heart pounded so intensely that her rib cage hurt. Light flashed on and off above the wall of the carrel. The attacker was searching on the other side of the room with a flashlight.

When the gunshot had been fired, she hadn't heard any cry of pain or the sound of a body dropping. Was Luke okay?

Only one set of footsteps padded on the carpet.

She crawled toward the opening in the carrel and peered out. Her eyes had adjusted to the darkness enough to make out the silhouettes of the office equipment and other furniture.

The footsteps stopped. No light shone through the room.

The silence settled around her as her throat tightened with fear. Her own breathing seemed unbearably loud.

She watched as a little light streamed through a window, where a shadow crossed it. The attacker was on the other side of the room.

She scrambled out and moved as quietly as she could back to just outside the elevator, where the initial attack had occurred. Her hand touched the vacuum cleaner where it had been left.

A flashlight clicked on several feet away. The attacker had stepped into the corner office on the opposite side of the building.

"Luke," she whispered.

His hand touched her shoulder and then grasped her fingers. Escaping in the elevator would be too risky. She didn't know if the malfunction had been caused by the assailant or not. He'd found a way to kill the electricity on the third floor. Maybe he had tampered with the elevator as well. If it had stopped once, it might happen again.

Staying close to the wall, she tugged on his hand and pulled him toward the stairs.

Footsteps rapidly approached. Luke let go of her hand. Another flash of light.

Gunfire. Two shots. Darkness.

In the flash of light, she saw the door to the stairwell. They were closer than she realized.

She reached out for the doorknob. She could feel Luke's body heat as he pressed close to her. She swung the door open as more gunfire echoed in the empty space. The shooter seemed to be guessing at where they were. Luke dared not fire back and give away their position.

They hurried down the first flight of stairs. Luke looked out the window of the landing. "My deputy's in the parking lot."

He grabbed Jillian's sleeve before she could take the flight of stairs that led down to the first floor.

"My deputy can help." He pulled out his phone and was pressing buttons. "The suspect is probably taking the elevator down and expecting to get at us on the first floor. Stay here where it's safe. We can take this guy in."

Luke was halfway down the stairs before he finished his sentence. He spoke into his phone. "Be advised, he's headed to the first floor. Entry code is 2465."

Luke opened the door to the first floor and stepped through. It eased shut, letting in a little light as Luke disappeared through it.

Jillian pressed against the wall and braced for the sound of gunfire. She hoped Luke caught the man after her. She listened for movement above her, but there was only silence. Silence and darkness. She was alone.

Luke stepped out onto the first floor, which had only one light on, just like when they'd entered. There must be a control panel for each floor. In the silence, the sound of the keypad being pressed and the door clicking open was audible. His deputy stepped inside, gun drawn, and pressed against the wall.

Luke surveyed the whole floor, not seeing any sign of the assailant. He wouldn't have been able to escape out the front door without being caught.

The mechanical hum of the elevator filled the empty space.

Luke moved toward it, seeking cover behind

a trash can. His deputy moved in as well, hiding in the shadows.

The elevator doors slipped open. He could just make out a dark figure pressed against the back wall. The door slid shut.

"He's going back up," Luke murmured.

"On it." The deputy moved toward the stairwell just as Jillian burst through the door. "I saw"

Luke rushed toward her, wrapping his arm around her as his deputy headed up the stairs. "Let's get you out of here."

He led her outside and toward the deputy's patrol car, which was closest to the building. A shot fired from above had them both dropping to the pavement. Luke covered Jillian's body with his own. He rolled away from her but kept his hand on her back before glancing over his shoulder.

The assailant must be shooting from the second floor.

"Run!" he yelled.

Both of them got to their feet. He turned with his weapon drawn to peer at the second-story windows. He couldn't see the attacker, but one of the windows was open.

Jillian was almost to the patrol car when another shot was fired at her. Luke shot back before retreating toward the car.

She flung the passenger side door open.

He opened the driver's side door and pulled

the radio. "He's on the second floor. Window, northwest corner."

"Headed down," the deputy radioed.

"I'll cover the first floor. No way can he escape." Luke dropped the radio and looked at Jillian. "Stay down."

He ran back toward the building, pressed the keypad and stepped inside. He took cover behind a counter and lifted his head to see above it. He was out of breath and his heart raged from the confrontation. His gaze moved back and forth between the stairwell and the elevator.

His phone buzzed and the deputy spoke. "Shell casings are on the floor, but he's not here."

"Keep looking, he's got to be somewhere in the building." Without hanging up, Luke checked the stairwell, then turned to watch the elevator.

His deputy's voice thundered out of the phone speaker. "He jumped from a different window. He's headed toward the patrol car."

Adrenaline flooded Luke's body as he sprinted toward the outside door. He needed to get to Jillian before the attacker did.

EIGHT

Jillian lifted her head just above the dashboard. The man dressed in black was headed right toward the patrol car. The keys were not in the ignition.

She pushed open the door, jumped out and ran toward Luke's truck. A shot fired behind her. Her heart was pounding by the time she reached for the driver's side door of the truck.

More gunfire. This time coming from just outside the building. Luke firing at the attacker had caused him to turn his attention away from Jillian and flee. The attacker exited the parking lot on foot. The darkness enveloped the man dressed all in black as he took the grassy slope into a ditch and up to the road. Luke's light blue jacket was visible as he sprinted across the grass toward the assailant.

The man would come out on the street above the office building. Luke had left the keys in the ignition of his truck. She could help catch this guy. She started the truck and headed toward the street closest to where the man would probably have to cross.

Jillian zoomed out of the parking lot and onto the road. Luke was running alongside her. He glanced over his shoulder and ran back to her, flinging open the passenger side door. "That way." He pointed toward a side street.

While she drove, he called his deputy. "Suspect is on foot, headed east on Dalmare Road."

She couldn't hear the deputy's muffled reply.

She turned on the street that Luke had indicated.

"Slow down." He scanned the cluster of trees and bushes.

An apartment building with only a few lit windows was three blocks away. She saw no sign of the attacker anywhere.

"Stop." Luke had already gripped the door handle. He tossed his phone in her direction. "Let my deputy know where I went."

Jillian picked up the phone and dialed the last number that had been punched in.

"Yes?" came the deputy's reply.

"This is Jillian. Luke is searching the trees just east of that first apartment building on Dalmare."

"I'm almost there," said the deputy, whom Luke had called Angus earlier.

She saw Luke's light-colored jacket for only a

moment before it disappeared into the shadows created by the brush and trees.

The deputy's patrol car skirted around the truck and parked off the road at an angle around the corner. He jumped out and headed into the brush a little farther up the road than where Luke had gone.

She took in a deep breath, trying to slow her heartbeat and find some calm. When she looked in the rearview mirror, a car went by on the road behind her. A light clicked off in the apartment building. Her heartbeat still thrummed in her ears.

She shrunk down in the seat and gazed up at a gossamer cloud floating toward the moon.

An explosive smacking sound jarred her back to reality. She stared through the windshield, barely able to make out the attacker as he raised his gun. He'd pounded on the hood of the truck so she would sit up straighter, so he could have a clean shot at her. A scream caught in her throat as she froze.

The man glanced off to the side as a shot exploded from the left. He dropped the arm that held the gun and then ran in the opposite direction he'd come. Both the deputy and Luke emerged in different spots from the bushes.

The deputy kept running in the direction the attacker had gone as Luke opened the door of the truck. She fell into his arms.

"I've got you," he said.

His soothing voice and the warmth of his arms comforted her. The reality that she had been only a second away from death made her shudder. He drew her closer. His chin brushed over the top of her head.

He held her for a long moment until she could take in a deep breath. "I'll sit behind the wheel and stay with you. I don't want to take the chance that he comes back this way."

She swung her legs around and scooted across the seat. "If you hadn't come out of those trees and fired at that man, I could've died."

"Don't let your mind go there." Luke was still out of breath from the pursuit. He rested his head against the back of the seat. "No more letting you out in the open even if it does draw him out."

He was right. That had been too close, and it terrified her. In the end she wasn't able to help Eloise anyway. The thought of another part of her life being ripped from her made her stomach do a somersault, but the man after her was relentless.

Confusion warred within her. "Maybe it would just be easier to leave Spring Meadow. Have WITSEC set me up somewhere else."

He nodded. "They certainly could, but I know how badly you want to stay here." Luke leaned forward in his seat. "We almost had him tonight. I'm sorry, Jillian."

The deputy emerged from the darkness, stepping out onto the road and shaking his head. He trotted back toward his car. Luke's phone rang just as the deputy pulled out. Jillian could only hear one side of the conversation, but it sounded like the deputy was going to continue to search for the suspect in his car.

Luke put the phone down and ran his fingers over his jaw.

"What are you thinking?" she said.

"It just seems odd to me that both times the guy finds you at work, he has a gun. But he was unarmed when he came into your house."

"I hadn't thought of that. His intent in breaking into the house was to scare me and to leave that message. But I suppose it's kind of risky. Why not bring the gun if you have it?"

Luke didn't answer, appearing lost in thought. "Come on," he said. "I'm taking you back to the farm. At least we know you're safe there."

She hoped that was true. As she stared out the window at the darkness, her heart grew heavy. She didn't want to lose the connections she'd built here, but it seemed it was being taken from her piece by piece.

Luke tried to focus on the road in front of him. Jillian was leaning toward leaving Spring Meadow. Why did that bother him?

The thought of losing her tonight had terrified him. He shouldn't feel so connected to her, yet he wanted to give her more than safety. He wanted her to be happy. She deserved that. He'd felt his heart warm toward her when they'd fed the animals last night. Not an emotion he'd experienced since he'd fallen in love with Maria in high school. But Jillian's situation was too precarious. She was in grave danger and could be leaving soon. A reminder that that people could be snatched out of your life as suddenly as a storm moved in across the prairie.

Whatever blossoming feelings had risen to the surface toward her, entertaining them would only lead to pain.

They returned to the office building to get Jillian's things, and then he drove back out to the farm. The house was quiet when they stepped inside. She turned to face him. "Are you going to feed the animals?"

"Part of my routine."

"I'll go with you." She stepped toward him with that earnest look on her face.

The thought of being alone with her in the quiet calm of night brought back the memory of holding her when the attacker had almost shot her. He was entranced by her strength and her vulnerability. In so many ways, she was already finding a way into his heart. He couldn't let that happen.

"I think it would be better if you stayed inside," he said.

"But that text showed that the stalker doesn't know where I'm hiding at. And he was on foot—he couldn't have tailed us back here. You said as much yourself that I was safe here."

As she stared up at him with those soft brown eyes, he felt his resistance melting. "Let's not take any chances."

"I'm not going to sleep. I'm just going to pace the floor. I might wake up your mother."

He tilted his head toward the ceiling and threw up his hands in surrender. "You don't give up, do you?"

She shrugged. "The truth is… I feel safer when I'm with you."

She seemed so exposed in that moment, and it had his resistance disappearing completely. He nodded, and they stepped out into the coolness of the autumn night. Stopping first to feed Princess, clean her stall and give her fresh hay. They worked together without talking. They walked the short distance to the barn where the alpacas and the pig were. Once inside, Luke's phone pinged with a text. He clicked the button to see that the message was from Angus.

No sign of him. He must have had a car stashed somewhere.

Luke replied: Good work. We'll keep an eye on our suspects from the hotel.

This second attack at the office seemed as vicious as the first, from what Jillian had said. The attacker was intent on killing Jillian and it had a high degree of premeditation. To lie in wait like the man had done suggested the work of a professional. The inconsistencies in the attacks troubled him.

Tomorrow was Luke's day off. He needed to get some sleep. He couldn't maintain this schedule for much longer. He'd thought the assailant would be in custody by now.

Jillian put the food down in front of Petunia the pig and then knelt to scratch her back. "You look concerned. Anything I should know about?"

He put his phone back in his pocket. "My deputy didn't catch the guy."

Jillian nodded but didn't say anything. She stroked the pig's hindquarters. "She's got a cut on her hip."

Luke moved toward her and knelt. "She probably brushed up against something sharp when my niece let her out during the day."

The cut looked deep, and when Jillian pressed around it, Petunia squealed in pain. "I could suture this if you have a first aid kit. At the very least, the wound needs to be cleaned out so it doesn't get infected."

Jillian continued to make soothing sounds as she stroked the pig's ears and jaw. Luke retrieved a first aid kit he'd put together for the other barn and handed it to her.

She flipped the kit open and peered inside. "What do we have to work with here?"

There was something relaxing about watching her clean and seal up the cut. He was struck by how quickly and deftly she worked while still taking a moment to sooth the animal. She'd been a nurse before she'd come into the program. He wondered if she missed it.

"All better." She patted the pig's belly. Petunia grunted and rubbed her snout on Jillian's shirt. Leaving a smear. Jillian laughed and rubbed the animal's ears.

"I think she likes you," he said. "You seem to have found your calling."

"Taking care of pigs?"

"Taking care of everyone and everything." He held her gaze for a moment, and her eyes rounded.

Petunia settled down into the hay.

"If something is hurting and I have the skill to make it better, it makes sense that I should step in, right? I will say that there is a limit to that. I shouldn't have risked my own safety to help Eloise. I think sometimes my compulsion to help gets out of hand."

"Right—you got to set boundaries." He was kneeling, facing her close enough that her floral perfume surrounded him. "It must be hard not to be able to be a nurse anymore. It seems like it was what you were born to do."

Jillian picked up a handful of straw and sifted it through her fingers, letting it fall to the dirt floor of the barn. Her voice was strained with emotion as she said, "You have no idea."

"I know what it is to have your life turned upside down. To lose the life that you thought you were going to have." His throat tightened. Why was he going here with her?

She met his gaze and shook her head. "What do you mean?"

He swallowed to try to get rid of the lump in his throat. "I was engaged when I was twenty. She died in a car wreck. We were going to take over the farm and run it together."

Warmth came into her eyes as her expression softened even more. "That's a lot to deal with at such a young age." She reached out and cupped her hand on his arm.

The look in her eyes drew him in. She understood in a way no one else did. His heart beat a little faster.

Watch yourself, Luke. It's too risky.

Seeking to break the connection between them, he turned away from her and stared at the wall.

When he glanced up, her gaze was unwavering. "Yeah, well. Life goes on, right?" He shifted away from her.

"I don't know, does it?" There was confusion in her voice.

He retreated toward the door with her question lingering in his mind. "I really need to get some sleep." The intense attraction rushing through him scared him. It was like he couldn't shut it down when he was around her.

She got up and joined him at the door. Then they walked back to the house in silence. The rhythm of their footsteps and the wind rustling tree branches were the only sounds of the night.

He opened the door to the house and moved to one side so she could go in first. They stood in the living room, where a lamp had been left on.

"I'm going to hit the sack," he said. "Tomorrow is my day off from policing, but that means I'll attend to all the farm stuff that has piled up. It will allow me to watch over you closer."

She nodded. "I think I'll make a cup of tea and to try to settle in. I'll do my best to be quiet."

"Mom's a pretty heavy sleeper, and so am I."

"Thank you for letting me go with you to feed the animals. I enjoy that."

He found himself wanting to stay in the warm glow of the moment, basking in the tenderness he saw in her eyes. But he pulled himself away and turned toward the stairs, dragging his tangled up feelings with him.

After he'd cleaned up and changed into pajamas, he stared out the window, listening as Jillian trod past his door.

He settled down to sleep. Sometime in the night, he was awakened by the glow of car headlights through the window. He rose and stared outside but didn't see anything, not even the shining of red taillights. His brother wouldn't be out at this hour, and there was only one other farm beyond theirs before the road dead-ended. It could just be his neighbor getting home late.

He watched the road for a long time.

Was it just a matter of time before the attacker figured out where Jillian was staying? Luke wouldn't let that happen. He had to catch this guy before he caught up to them.

NINE

Jillian spent the morning helping Charlotte get her supplies ready to load in the car in order to travel to set up classes with some small fabric and craft stores. After much persuading, Luke had convinced his mother to leave the property for a few days, and Jillian was glad that Charlotte would be out of town so she wouldn't be in danger. She was also surprised at how well she'd slept. Since returning to work was not an option for now, maybe she would finally be able to sleep at night. Something about being out in the country seemed to help her insomnia. Maybe it had something to do with knowing that Luke was close by and ready to protect her as well.

When she set supplies by the door for Charlotte to carry out, she caught a glimpse of Luke walking toward a barn with a toolbox.

Once Charlotte drove away, Jillian was left in a silent house. She was resigned to the fact that she needed to stay inside and out of sight. She read and worked on cutting some fabric Charlotte had asked her to do.

Staying out of sight behind the curtain, she peeked from an upstairs window. Another man, who must be Luke's brother, ran the vegetable stand.

Later in the day, a knock on the door startled her as she stood in the kitchen chopping vegetables for a casserole. She could at least help by making sure Luke and whoever was hungry had a hot meal at the end of the day. It seemed to her that Luke really never gave himself a day off. If he wasn't policing, he was dealing with farm issues.

She moved toward the door but hesitated. She pulled back the curtain by the side window. A woman with two small children stood on the porch.

Jillian swung open the door.

"I'm sorry to bother you, but we're ready to pay for our vegetables and there's no one at the stand." The woman indicated the basket she held and the smaller buckets each child held filled with corn and squash.

"You walked all the way over here." When she peered over the woman's shoulder, there was no sign of Luke's brother or Luke. "Oh, Matt must have stepped away. Let me go see if I can find him."

There was a substantial stretch of yard between the house and where the u-pick stand was. She could see a couple people in the field picking vegetables.

By the time she made it to the food stand, her heart was beating faster. She felt exposed. She still saw no sign of Luke or Matt. The setup at the stand looked fairly straight forward. There was a scale and a metal box that must hold the cash. A sign on the front of the stand read, "Cash or local check only." The prices of each vegetable were listed as well.

"Here, why don't I just do this for you?"

While she weighed the produce and took the woman's money, another car pulled up and two men got out. They looked like father and son. Both were holding small totes that must be for hauling vegetables.

The woman with the children was pulling away in her car when Jillian felt a hand on her shoulder.

She startled and turned to face Matt. Up close, he resembled Luke in terms of the slant of his eyes and the strong jaw, but he looked less weighed down by life even though he was the older brother. There was a brightness to his expression that Luke didn't have.

"Aren't you supposed to stay in the house?"

"A woman knocked on the door. She wanted

help paying for her produce. I put the money in the metal box."

"I just stepped away for a minute to move the sprinklers. Sorry about that. Usually, people just leave the money on the table or wait around. It's pretty informal. Most people are trustworthy."

"You've got a nice little business here," she said.

"It's not much of a business. We're lucky to break even."

"Why keep doing it then?"

"Habit. Mostly it's Luke who wants to keep this going. I try to honor his wishes, but honestly, things might need to change soon. My wife is almost finished with her teaching degree."

"What does that mean?"

Matt shrugged. "Not sure. Would like to have the option of moving if she finds a job in another town. I can do my job as an agricultural loan officer almost anywhere in the state." Apparently, both Matt and Charlotte were ready to leave the farm.

"So, why not just leave Luke to run the place since he's the one who's attached to it?"

"You see how this works. It's not a one-man operation."

Another car pulled up.

"I should probably get back to the house." She walked the distance back to the farmstead with what Matt had told her buzzing through her mind. She wondered why Luke wanted to hold on to the farm when it seemed like more of a burden than a blessing.

She approached the door and turned the knob. In her haste to help the woman and her children, she'd left the door unlocked.

That wasn't very smart. She looked around hoping to catch sight of Luke but didn't see him.

Feeling uneasy, she stepped inside where she was greeted by silence. Without being able to say why, something about the house felt…disturbed. She turned and locked the door. She hurried to the kitchen to get her phone on the counter. Everything in the kitchen looked exactly like she'd left it.

Still, she couldn't let go of her fear. She pressed in Luke's number.

"Yes." His voice sounded strained like he was walking briskly or moving something around.

"I left the house and forgot to lock the door. Everything seems alright but…"

"I'll be there in five minutes. Stay close to the door and keep it locked."

Luke showed up a few minutes later and walked through the house with his gun drawn. He returned to the living room where she waited.

"All clear," he said. "I'm going to hang closer

to the house for the rest of the day. There's some stuff on the nearby barn I can deal with."

"I don't mean to keep you from your work."

Light shone in his eyes. "It's okay." He stepped toward her. "My primary job is to watch out for you."

After Luke left, she walked through the house up to her room, pushing on the door and letting it ease open. Marmy lay on the bed, but there was no sign of George. She searched the house and called his name. He may have found a new hiding spot.

She finished the casserole and cleaned up the kitchen. She looked again for George, checking behind the washer and dryer and in the craft room where the old cat still slept.

A scratching at the front door alerted her. After twisting the dead bolt, she swung it open and looked down at the porch. "George."

She gathered the cat into her arms as her heart revved up a notch. No way would he have gone out of the house unless he'd been scared or carried out.

The cars parked by the u-pick stand had all left. She stared out at the gray sky and the quiet of a seemingly empty farm.

She stroked the cat's head and drew him closer to her chest. Her mouth was dry and her throat tight. Should she call Luke again? "You

had a fright, huh? Let's get you settled down."
She moved up the stairs to her room and placed
George on the bed where Marmy lounged. She
reached for her phone.

From the upstairs window, she saw Luke running up the hill toward the barn where the animals were as if something had alarmed him.

She watched as a man moved from behind one
building to another shed. His quick steps and his
head swiveling from side to side suggested he
didn't want to be seen.

Her chest got tight. That guy didn't act like one
of the u-pick customers who'd decided to casu-
ally poke around the farm.

And she could no longer see Luke.

The man moved to the tractor and picked
something out of the open toolbox, stalking toward where Luke had gone.

Jillian's heart pounded against her rib cage as
she pressed in Luke's number and took in a jagged breath while she listened as the phone rang
and rang. But he didn't pick up. Was she too late?

Her phone pinged and a text appeared. She
pressed the button to read it.

You are mine and only mine.

The attacker was here on the property. She had
to warn Luke. She rushed down the stairs, out
the door and into the night.

* * *

Luke had hurried up the hill when he saw Princess wandering around. Had someone let her out of the barn?

"Here you go, old girl." His feelings of unease only increased as he led her back to her stall. He moved to pull his phone out to check on Jillian, but it wasn't there. He must have left it in the other barn.

He whirled around when he heard footsteps behind him.

Jillian rushed in. "There's a man stalking around the property. I think he was in the house earlier."

Now he knew why Princess had been let out, to lure him away from the barn that was closest to the house.

"I could see from the upstairs window. He picked up a tool and was moving toward where you had gone. I think he was going to hurt you."

Something that would have left Jillian vulnerable. "Give me your phone so I can call for backup." It would take his deputies half an hour to get here. "We need to get you secured in the house."

She moved to hand him her phone.

A thudding noise at the door caused them both to pivot. Luke stalked toward the sliding wooden door and pushed. "Someone slid the wooden bar in place that locks this from the outside."

He slammed his shoulder against it twice, but it didn't budge.

Princess stomped the ground and lifted her head up and down. Noise from the loft caused them both to look up.

Smoke rose from the hay stored there.

He watched as the flickering orange strands of the flames increased in size. The attacker must have thrown something flammable on the hay. The barn filled with smoke as Princess kicked at her stall.

"We have to go up and out," Luke said. "He must have used a ladder to throw something flammable in the barn. We can get down that way."

The fire spread quickly through the loft, eating up the highly combustible hay. They both coughed. They had no other choice.

They ran toward the ladder that led to the loft. He stepped aside so Jillian could go up first. The smoke grew thicker, searing his lungs and throat. Bent over and coughing, Jillian made her way to the window.

He peered over her shoulder. There was usually a ladder, but it had been pushed to the ground.

The heat of the fire pressed on his back. The smoke stung his eyes and had grown so thick that Jillian was nearly invisible, even though she was only feet from him. "I'll lower you as far as I can."

"I'll put the ladder up for you," she said.

Heat pressed against his legs and back. Jillian put her feet through the window. He gripped her arms at the wrist and leaned as far out of the window as he could.

Below him, Princess banged and kicked at her stall, rearing up and stomping the ground. The noises she made were that of an animal who was terrified. His heart clenched. He wished he had time to release her, but he had to get Jillian out first. Then he'd go back for his horse.

Jillian dropped to the ground taking a moment to recover from the fall before reaching for the ladder. He was already partially hanging out the window when she propped the ladder against the wall. Smoke swirled around him. His throat felt like fingernails had been scraped across it.

He put his foot on the first rung of the ladder and climbed down. Once he hit the ground, he hurried around the side of the barn to the front, then lifted the wooden bar that held the door in place. The lower level of the barn was completely filled with smoke. He could hear Princess's frightened whinny as she kicked the side of her stall.

His eyes watered as he made his way toward

the noise and felt for the lever that would open her stall. Coughing, he reached up to grip her mane and led her out toward the door. Once outside, he let go of her. She took off running but slowed several yards away. She'd come back on her own when she calmed down.

Jillian was not on this side of the barn. He'd assumed she would follow him but wait outside while he got the horse out. Tension knotted the back of his neck when he ran around to the side of the building where the ladder was on the ground. She wasn't there either. He said her name and then shouted it as he circled around the entire burning barn.

A new kind of fear descended on him as he ran in a larger circle looking everywhere for her.

He sprinted back toward the other barn to retrieve his phone just as it rang. He picked up without looking at the number, hoping to hear Jillian's voice.

"I saw the fire. I've called the fire department." The voice was his brother's.

"Did…did Jillian come over there to tell you about it?"

"Jillian's not here. Why?"

"Call the police too. She's been taken."

TEN

Jillian caught flashes of the trees around her as her captor dragged her into the forest. He held one hand over her mouth and the other arm pressed hard against her stomach.

"You're supposed to be with me, Jillian."

Though the voice was filled with a mixture of anger and hurt, it sounded familiar. Just like before, the man wore a covering over his face.

She struggled to break free, but his hold on her was unyielding. Every time she twisted her body, he squeezed harder against her belly. She tried a different tactic, becoming very still and not resisting him. Maybe that would make him let his guard down.

His grip remained tight. His hand was pressed so hard against her mouth that her neck was bent back.

All she could see around her were deciduous trees with only a few leaves left on the branches. The darkness was disorienting. She wasn't even sure where she was on the farm.

"If I can't have you, no one can." He spoke between gasps for air, but the note of menace in his voice was not lost on her.

She knew that voice. Roger from the coffee place. It wasn't someone from out of town. When he'd seen her with Luke and they'd pretended to be involved, that must have set him off. And allowed him to figure out where she was staying.

Though her heart was beating out of control, she tried to relax her body even more. She took in a deep breath, hoping by not resisting him, he would relax his hold on her.

This time, the pressure on her mouth and stomach let up a little. She didn't seek to break free or struggle in any way.

Don't fight him. He might let his guard down.

What was his plan anyway? He must've parked his car somewhere out of view.

Even if he intended to kill her right here, the car must be close enough to provide a way of escape.

He leaned close to her ear. His voice held a sickly sweet quality. "I thought you loved me, Jillian. I loved you. I saw you every night and once I found out about your show, I never missed it."

He must have been watching her for some time and seen her through her window doing the podcast or maybe he'd even been in her house and looked at her computer files to find out the name of the show. How else could he have known it was her? The realization caused her to taste bile in her throat.

She made a noise, trying to answer back, but he kept his hand on her mouth. She continued the passive rag-doll act.

He seemed to relax more once he'd caught his breath from the initial struggle. "But you chose the sheriff, didn't you?" The rage returned to his voice.

It was now or never. Her body went from marshmallow to hardened steel in a nanosecond. She twisted away. Roger reached out for her arm, but she yanked it away and took off running. Branches scratched her face. She saw no end to the forest.

The crunch of dried leaves on the ground told her he was close behind her. She sprinted faster, weaving through the trees.

He caught her by the back of her collar and slammed her head against a tree trunk.

"Try and get away from me, huh?"

Her knees buckled as trees and the night sky spun around her.

She must have collapsed and lost consciousness for a few seconds. Her awareness returned when she realized Roger was on top of her, resting his knee on her stomach with his hands wrapped around her neck.

His white teeth shone in the darkness and his rage was palpable. She whipped her head side to side, scratching and clawing at his hands.

Air. She needed air. White spots filled her field of vision. She reached up and dragged her fingernails down his arm. His hands suctioned even tighter around her neck.

Sirens sounded in the distance.

He decreased the pressure on her neck and turned his head sideways toward the noise. The inattention allowed her to take in a sharp breath.

She reached up to slap his hands away, but he grabbed her hair and yanked.

"You're coming with me."

He forced her to her feet. His hold on her hair was so strong it caused her to bend toward him to relieve the pain. His other hand clamped onto her arm. He pushed her through the trees to a flat area, where a car was parked.

Far in the distance, more sirens wailed.

Once she got into that car, she was a dead woman.

Despite the pain it caused her, she angled her body and kicked Roger in the shin. He yelped and let go of her. But seconds later, he had her again. A car door opened, and she was pushed through it. When he dragged her legs into the car, she thought she might vomit. He slammed the back door shut.

Another door opening and closing. She slumped against the back seat. As her vision faded, she noticed a hammer on the front passenger seat. That must have been what Roger had taken from Luke's toolbox, intending to use it as a weapon. The car engine hummed.

The last thing she heard were the tires rolling on the dirt road before she passed out.

As Luke walked the front end of property through the rows of corn, he couldn't shake the fear that plagued his thoughts. He knew they had only a small window to find Jillian alive. The fire trucks from the rural fire department had arrived, but it would take close to a half hour for the police to get here unless one of his deputies was out on a call close by.

Matt and Tasha had agreed to search the backside of the property while the firefighters dealt with the barn and he searched the front of the property.

The sound of a car rolling by on the road caused him to lift his head. The older model vehicle wasn't anything his neighbor drove. His neighbor, who was a senior citizen, wouldn't be out at this hour anyway. He could just make out the driver furtively glancing at the farm and then speeding up. He'd seen that car before. It had tried to run him down outside Jillian's house.

The hairs on the back of his neck prickled. His heart beat a little faster.

Jillian was in that car.

He ran through the cornfield back to where to his truck was. Grateful that he always kept the keys in the ignition when he parked at the farm, he jumped in and started the engine.

He sped toward the road that led back into town, pressing the accelerator to the floor. Within a few minutes, he had the older car in his sights just as it rounded a curve.

He hung back, hoping the driver wouldn't realize he was being followed. When Luke got around the curve, there was no sign of the car.

Luke slowed down. He had to have turned off somewhere. Luke executed a U-turn on the empty road and backtracked, driving slowly. He caught the glint of metal nearly hidden by some brush. He cranked the wheel and rolled over the uneven ground.

The car stood in the moonlight. He stopped his truck and pushed open the door. No movement came from within the car or around the outside of it. The guy couldn't have gotten far. There hadn't been time to grab his gun, he realized as he stepped out of the truck.

He tuned into his surroundings as he approached the car. His footsteps padded lightly on the short grass until he reached the car and peered into the driver's side window. Empty. He stepped toward the back seat and reached to open the door when he heard a twig snap behind him. He whirled, just as something hard swung to-ward his head.

He'd managed to dodge it in time so that it was just a glancing blow. Still, pain radiated though his head and neck as he whirled around to face the man who'd hit him with a hammer. He rec-ognized the man. Roger from the coffee hut. He lifted the hammer to strike another blow.

Luke lunged at him, and his fist collided with the man's jaw. He was still disoriented, and the blow wasn't hard enough to knock Roger down. Shaking his head, the attacker stepped back and took off running toward the trees. Luke tried to ignore the pain from being struck on the side of the head. But he felt dizzy as he pursued Roger. He lost sight of him when the forest grew thick. He slowed to a jog, listening for footsteps. He didn't want to be jumped by the guy. Another smartly laid blow from that hammer could do him in.

A rustle of noise directed him to turn. The trees thinned, and he could hear the rushing hum of a creek. He saw the man who was mostly shadow as he neared the water. Luke sprinted with all the power and strength he had left in his legs.

He leapt on top of Roger. They both fell in the

water as they wrestled. Roger broke free from Luke's grasp and crawled halfway up the bank. The man flipped over and swung the hammer at Luke again. Luke dodged the blow fully this time, gripped the man's wrist and twisted until he dropped the hammer. With water dripping off both of them, Luke grabbed the man's shirt front and pulled him to his feet as he stood up himself.

"I think you're coming with me." Luke spoke between breaths.

Roger resisted, turning his face away and twisting his body. Luke grabbed hold of his shirt front with both hands.

"She was meant to be with me," Roger sneered.

"Where is she? Where is Jillian?" Fear pierced him like a blade through his heart. What if she was already dead?

"Wouldn't you like to know?"

"Don't try anything."

The man yelped as Luke twisted his arm behind his back at an awkward angle and shoved him forward. He kept one hand on Roger's arm and the other on the back of Roger's collar as he pushed him through the trees to where their cars were.

Keeping his eye on Roger, he phoned Deputy Walters, who must be getting close to the property by now. She answered. He gave her his location.

Though he was plagued by thoughts of where Jillian was and what might have happened to her, he couldn't leave Roger unattended and risk his trying to escape.

After restraining Roger with some rope, he checked around the man's car. His heart stopped when the glint of bright-colored clothing caught his eye. Concealed by some brush, Jillian lay in the grass face down and motionless. His chest squeezed tight.

He barely registered the lights of Angie's squad car when he reached to gather Jillian into his arms. Though it was hard to see in darkness, he didn't notice any sign of her having been beaten with the hammer. She was limp in his arms, but he found a pulse when he placed his fingers on her neck.

Angie had already approached Roger to take him into custody.

Luke's heart raced as he lifted Jillian. The bruising and cut on her forehead caused the panic to dig its claws into his psyche.

Angie stopped and turned as she led a now cuffed Roger to the squad car. "Never would have guessed it was this guy. Stanley Reese left town this morning. We can't find Jon Wilson. You gonna be all right with her?"

He pressed his fingers against the cool skin of Jillian's cheek. "I need to get her to the hospital." His voice was hoarse, and his throat had gone completely dry.

Roger turned to look at him.

Luke wanted to shake the other man and to scream, "What have you done to her?"

"She should have been mine." Roger spoke in almost a whisper.

Though he couldn't read Roger's expression at this distance in the dark, his body language, the rounded shoulders and bent head, suggested defeat.

As Angie pulled out, Luke hurried to his truck and placed Jillian on the passenger seat, where she slumped forward. His own head was hurting by the time he got behind the wheel. Calling an ambulance would take too long. It was up to him to get her to a place where she could get medical attention.

He needed to get her to the hospital. As he drove with the headlights cutting a swath of illumination through the darkness, he thought about the twisted irony of Jillian no longer being in danger only to perhaps lose her life if he didn't act quickly.

He spoke out loud. "You're not going to die. Not on my watch."

He couldn't imagine a world without her in it.

ELEVEN

When she opened her eyes, the first thing Jillian was aware of was a throbbing headache. The second thing that registered was the warm calloused hand covering her own.

"Hey, sleepy head." Luke's baritone voice filled the air around her.

Despite the intense pain in her head, she took some comfort in knowing he was so close.

"Roger…?"

"We got him. He's in custody."

She stared at the sterile white ceiling as relief spread through her. She heard beeping noises. She must be at the hospital. "It's over then."

He leaned closer. Despite the pain, she turned her head and looked into his eyes. "He's locked in a jail cell. You can stay in Spring Meadow." The faintest of smiles graced his face.

"How long have I been out?" It had just started to get dark when Roger had taken her.

"It's early morning."

The reality of what he said sank in. "I can go back to my home and my job?" A sadness she didn't understand washed through her. She'd go back to a life that was busy but without deep connection, and to a job that was not overly meaningful. Wasn't that what she'd wanted? So much of not wanting to leave Spring Meadow had been driven by not wanting to have to start all over again now that she knew how hard it was to become a new person in another town.

"I don't think you should be working for at least a few days, honey." A nurse had come through the door. "That's a pretty severe knock you got on your head. Doctor is concerned there might be some delayed side effects."

"Ah, yes, sometimes with a concussion there can be unexpected unconsciousness days afterward," said Jillian.

"Yes," said the nurse. "You've had some medical training?"

The injury was making her let her guard down. "Must have read it in a book somewhere."

"You're going to need someone to keep an eye on you." The nurse stepped closer to Luke. "You both are. Since you both got knocked on the head."

"We can keep an eye on each other." He leaned

toward Jillian again. "Doc says I shouldn't be on shift for at least twenty-four hours either. I got a bump on the side of my head too."

They would be spending some more time together. That wouldn't be such a bad thing. But once they were both in the clear for not losing consciousness from the head injury, they'd have no reason to be together. Why was she thinking about that anyway? After Gregory, hadn't she decided to let go of the idea of dating. Although it was clear to her that Luke was nothing like Gregory, being involved with someone in witness protection was precarious. Luke had sacrificed enough. "Roger hit you too?"

"Yes," said Luke.

The nurse moved toward the door. "I'll leave you two alone. Doctor should sign the release order shortly."

Less than half an hour later, they called Matt and his wife to come get them since Luke shouldn't be driving for at least a day. They rode in the van with Tasha and the two girls while Matt drove Luke's truck back. Tasha and her daughters carried most of the conversation while Jillian was lost in thought.

As the van rolled down the road, something was bothering her that seemed to be just out of reach of her comprehension. The head injury was affecting her ability to put thoughts together.

When she tuned back to the conversation in the car, Tasha was talking about finishing her teaching degree in December.

"And then we're going to move, right?" said Tasha's older daughter from the back seat.

From the back seat where she sat with the two girls, Jillian watched Luke's shoulder twitch and Tasha give him a nervous glance. Evidence of the tension in the family over the farm.

"We don't know what's going to happen," said Tasha. "It all depends on where mommy gets a job."

Tasha dropped them off in front of the farmhouse. There was a Closed sign hung across the u-pick stand.

Matt showed up a few minutes later with Luke's truck.

"Thanks, Matt. I know this is going to make you late for work."

Matt offered his brother a wave. "We'll deal with it. Got to get Tasha and the girls into town for school and classes."

Matt got into the car with Tasha who turned the van around and headed back up the road that led to Spring Meadow.

Princess was in the front yard not too far from the house. "Guess I'll have to put her in the barn with Petunia. The alpacas can stay in the corral."

Luke stared off into the distance at the barn that was now just an ashen mass.

"Pretty big loss, huh?" she said.

He shook his head. "Been losing this farm in bits and pieces for years."

She wanted to ask him why he was the lone holdout for selling the farm. Why was he hanging on to it when his mother and brother were ready to let it go? The question seemed cruel though especially, after the loss of the barn. "I don't suppose you can rebuild?"

"There's no money for it. Insurance won't place much value on an old structure like that." Princess had already started to lumber toward him. He waved at Jillian and headed toward the old horse.

Jillian stepped inside the house. Marmy rose to greet her from the couch where she'd been lounging. She got the cats their food and filled their water dish. When she looked out the window, she saw Luke leading an uncooperative alpaca toward a fenced-in area.

She might as well go out and help him. She needed to check on how Petunia was healing anyway. She stepped outside, enjoying the sense of freedom she felt. She still couldn't process that Roger was behind all the violence of the last few days especially the attacks at the office.

After helping Luke with the second alpaca,

they both stood sideways facing each other, each with an arm resting on the fence. The morning sun had just started to warm things up.

"Thanks for your help." Light came into Luke's eyes.

"My pleasure. I like working with the animals. I think Petunia's cut will heal up nicely."

He reached out to touch the bandaged gash on Jillian's forehead. "Hope that heals up."

His touch sent a charge of electricity through her. Her eyes held his. There was a glow to his features that she hadn't seen before. A magnetic pull caused her to take a step toward him.

"I'm glad you're going to be able to stay in Spring Meadow." He leaned toward her. His eyes searching hers.

"Me too," she said.

Her lips parted slightly as her heart fluttered. Then he pressed his mouth against hers. She reached up to rest her hand against his cheek. When he pulled away after a long moment, the sun felt even warmer on her skin as she looked into his eyes. She'd been longing for that kiss.

His phone made a pinging noise, shattering the moment between them. With an apologetic smile, he pulled his cell from his pocket and stared at it. "It's my mom. I'll let it go to voice mail." His face seemed to soften with affection.

But his words had her snagging on something,

causing her to shift gears. "Voice mail." The connection she couldn't quite make earlier coalesced in her brain. "Voice."

His eyebrows furrowed. "What are you talking about?"

Her heart beat a little faster as the realization sank in. "Roger's voice and the voice from that first phone call when I was at work were two different voices."

She watched his expression change. "Two different men. One who carried a gun and one who did not." He nodded. "That makes sense. Something about the inconsistencies in the attacks seemed off to me."

Her muscles tensed as panic washed through her. "Luke, I'm still not safe."

An odd zinging noise surrounded her. Luke leapt toward her, covering her body with his and taking her to the ground. Before she felt the dirt, a percussive boom filled the air.

Someone was shooting at them with a rifle.

Luke lifted his head and scanned the area, trying to figure out where the shooter was. Mostly likely the hill on the other side of the road. A skilled shooter with a good rifle had tremendous range. This guy appeared to be that.

The alpacas ran around the corral, banging against the metal fence as their hooves pounded.

His arm was still across the Jillian's back.

Another shot was fired, kicking up dirt only feet from where they were.

He rolled onto his side facing Jillian. "Get to the far side of the shed. Stay low. Run in spurts."

Jillian nodded and burst to her feet, half crawling and half walking. He followed. A third shot was fired before he got to the far side of the shed, which would give them some cover.

Leaning his back against the aged wood of the shed, Luke pulled his phone out of his pocket and called dispatch. He didn't give her time to say hello.

"We're at the farm and we're being shot at."

Mary Ellen responded, "I don't understand. The suspect is sitting in a jail cell."

"No time to explain. Are Angie or Chris close?"

"Angie's at the station and Chris is on a call the other side of town."

"Tell Angie to get here as fast as she can." He clicked the disconnect button.

He and Jillian were both out of breath from running, not to mention the events of the night. They needed rest. She gazed at him. Her expression held a question.

What should they do next?

How long were they safe behind this shed before the shooter decided to move in to get a shot at them? They were alone out here. It would be half an hour before Angie arrived. They had to play offense to scare the gunman off before he could line up another shot.

Luke leaned around the side of the shed. He could just make out movement on the hill as the man ran from one sheltered area to another.

"I have a rifle in my truck." With his eyes, he traced the path he would have to go to get to his truck, the places he could take cover.

She grabbed his arm. "I'm going with you."

The shooter was already getting closer. She'd be safer with him than if he left her by herself. He nodded. "Stay close to me."

He ran toward the first place that provided cover, an old tractor. No shots were fired at them. The shooter must still be working his way toward them. He would have to stop to line up a shot. Now was the time to get to that truck.

He pointed at the barn where Princess was. They ran to the back of it and circled around. Though he peered out, the house blocked his view of the hill. They had one more stretch to cover before they reached the truck.

He crouched and moved toward a burn pile. Jillian pressed close to his back. He stood up, preparing to run the final yards to the truck.

A shot echoed around them and they both hit the ground. His heart pounded as he lay on his stomach. Jillian's shoulder pressed against his. The shooter had moved in fast. He was probably still across the road but on the flatter part of the land. The shooter knew they were behind the burn pile.

"I have to try to figure out where he's at and if he's on the move. Stay here."

Luke crawled soldier-style out on his stomach on the opposite side of the burn pile from where they'd previously tried to make a run for it. The adrenaline dump from the threat made him alert as his heartbeat thrummed in his ears.

He saw no movement across the road. Though the land was flat, there was tall grass and brush where a man could hide. Jillian crawled closer to him but was still hidden behind the burn pile.

He had to assume the shooter was in a position to get off another shot. He moved back toward the shelter of the burn pile. Crouching, he sat back on his feet and picked up a piece of metal and a small block of wood. He grabbed a branch that had some weight to it, drawing the object close to his stomach.

"What are you doing?"

"If this guy has any kind of sniper training, which I suspect he does, judging from the way he's setting up his shots, he'll react to movement." He handed her the objects. "Toss these out that way. One after the other. Even if he doesn't shoot at them, his attention will be off of us for a second." He pointed away from their position. "Then follow me."

She took the objects. He moved to the other side of the burn pile and looked over his shoulder. Their best chance was him getting to his rifle as quickly as possible to return fire. The first object hit the ground. Then the next. A shot zinged through the air. He took off running. Jillian was beside him within a second.

He positioned himself so his body shielded her from where the shooter was.

They were within yards of the truck before the shooter reoriented and took aim at them. Jillian crouched by the back wheel well while he opened his truck and reached to grab his rifle off the rack.

He steadied it by placing the barrel on the rim of the truck bed and then peered through the scope, moving it to have a sweeping view of the grass across the road. He saw no sign of the shooter, who must have moved in closer.

It was a short sprint to the house, but without knowing where the shooter was, he couldn't risk it.

"He's in the cornfield." Jillian's voice filled with panic. "I saw his head bob up."

The shooter had gotten across the road and was

even closer to the house. Near enough for Jillian to see him without a scope.

Jillian burst to her feet and ran toward the front of the truck.

Still holding the rifle, Luke crouched as Jillian swept past him. The first shot went through the passenger side window where he'd left the door open when he'd gotten his weapon. It left a hole but didn't shatter the glass.

The second shot left a burning sensation on his shoulder. The bullet had grazed him. He reached the front of the truck, where Jillian had pressed her back against the bumper.

Her chest moved up and down with the intensity of her breathing. "What now?"

His mind raced. "Make a run for the house."

The shooter would only have to move in a short distance to get a shot at them. She darted toward the porch stairs. The first shot hit one of the pillars on the porch. Jillian stayed low and crawled up the steps. He was right behind her. She reached up to twist the doorknob and they both crawled in.

A shot went through the window. Glass shards sprayed across the floor. On her hands and knees, Jillian moved toward the shelter of an easy chair.

He took up a position by the window that had just been shot out. He placed the barrel of the gun on the windowsill and then lifted his head just high enough to see outside. He caught movement as the guy dove behind a bush. The shooter was closing in.

Still crouching, Luke moved toward the door and clicked the dead bolt in place.

Jillian angled her head from behind the easy chair. "This time, they really have come for me, haven't they?"

She'd spoken the thought that had been on his mind from the moment the first shot had been fired at them. This man was aiming to kill. The inconsistencies in the nature of the attacks now made sense. The mafia had found Jillian.

TWELVE

Jillian's heart was still pounding from running to get into the house. She couldn't wrap her mind around what had just happened and what it meant for her future.

From the moment she'd agreed to go into WIT-SEC, she knew that this day might come. Her life here was over. If they got out of this alive, she couldn't stay in Spring Meadow.

Luke moved from one window to the next. Peering out and aiming his rifle but not taking a shot. When he looked over his shoulder at her, the concern she saw in his expression helped calm her frayed nerves. "You all right?"

"As good as can be expected." It was hard to get a deep breath in. It felt like an anvil had been placed on her chest. She shook herself free of the racing thoughts. Now was not the time to think about her future. They were under siege.

Luke turned his attention back to the window. They'd shared a kiss only moments before her world had been blown to pieces. Luke had thought she would be staying in Spring Meadow when he kissed her. The whole thing felt surreal. The safety she'd experienced knowing Roger was caught had been short-lived. She'd wanted Luke's kiss, wanted to think she could have something like a normal life.

Luke turned and pressed his back against the wall, the rifle held diagonally across his chest. He checked his phone. "Angie is still at least twenty minutes out. I need to call her and warn her about where the shooter is."

Jillian was so consumed with fear she only heard parts of Luke's phone call to his deputy.

She lifted her head slightly, trying to see out the window. She had a partial view of the truck and the cornfield in the distance but didn't see the man with the rifle anywhere. "What do we do? Wait him out?"

"I'd like to take him into custody." Luke turned and tilted his head toward the window. His voice held a forceful tone that she hadn't heard before. "Once my deputy gets here, that might be a possibility." He turned his head back toward the window. "Not sure if I have that kind of time, though."

The patch of red on the top part of his shoulder caused her to gasp. "You were hit." Her stomach twisted into a tight knot as she moved toward him.

He held up his palm toward her, indicating she needed to stay in place. "Just grazed. I'll be all right."

"Are you sure? Let me take a look at it."

"It's fine." Again, his voice held an intensity that told her not to persist. He turned his attention to the window again. "Why don't you go upstairs to your room, lock the door and stay away from the windows?"

What was he planning?

Crouching, she moved toward the stairs. Her body was tense from the danger that surrounded them as she put her foot on the first stair. Another shot came through the shattered window. She screamed when the top of the newel on the banister fell to the floor just as she was about to place her hand on it.

She dropped and rolled across the floor to the couch.

Luke half stood and then glared back at the staircase. "He must have repositioned to get that kind of a shot."

Her heart pounded as she took in shallow breaths.

"He's closer than I realized." Luke edged toward the other window, lifted his rifle and fired a shot. "He's by the truck."

The shooter was only yards from the house.

Fear permeated every cell of her being as she scooted around to the far side of the couch. Her hands dug into the fabric of the arm. Another shot was fired into the living room. The boom of the bullet was loud enough to make her ears ring.

Her body was shaking as she pressed against the side of the couch bent into a C-shape, holding her hands over her ears. She peered around the back of the sofa. Even taking in a breath was laborious.

Luke opened the unshattered window and fired two shots. Each one caused her to flinch.

Straightening her body, she lifted her head above the arm of the couch.

A tense silence shrouded the room while Luke remained poised to fire another shot. He peered through his scope, moving the barrel of the rifle a millimeter at a time. Then lifted his head from the scope.

The seconds ticked by as he focused on whatever he was seeing outside.

He pulled his rifle back down across his body as light came into his eyes. He signaled for her to stay put. He crawled across the living room floor into the kitchen. She heard the kitchen door open and shut.

Luke was taking a huge risk by going outside,

but he must be calculating where he could go to get a clean shot at the sniper.

Staying low to not be seen from the living room windows, she made her way toward the kitchen, hoping to look out a window in there.

She cringed when she heard a rifle shot and then another coming from a different direction.

The silence that followed caused the blood in her veins to freeze.

Luke had taken up a position at the corner of the house and lifted his rifle using his hand and the strap to brace it. He prepared to pull the trigger. He tilted his head so half his face would be visible if the shooter looked his way. He needed to see his target.

The next few seconds were a blur. He saw the shooter on the move. A bullet whizzed past him, taking a piece of wood out of the siding on the house. He fired a return shot.

He was out of bullets. The internal magazine only held five shots. The rifle was useless. The ammunition was in his truck.

The next noise he heard chilled him to the bone. The shooter's footsteps pounded on the wooden floorboards of the porch. He heard the sound of more breaking glass. Terror gripped Luke's heart.

The shooter was trying to get inside to get at

Jillian by crawling through the window because the door was locked. He might be conserving ammo. Otherwise, he would have shot his way in.

Heart pounding, Luke hurried through the side door that led into the kitchen. After propping the rifle against the counter, he braced against a wall and worked his way toward the living room. He could hear the receding footsteps of the shooter as he searched the main floor.

Jillian must have hidden somewhere. He prayed she'd had time to get upstairs. He heard a cat's irritated yowl. It sounded like the shooter was in his mom's craft room. Luke ran across the living room floor, keeping his steps as light as possible.

Marmy stood at the top of the stairs and yowled as he made his way up. The sound made him cringe. When he glanced down the stairs, the shooter had come back out into the living room. Luke ducked out of the way to avoid being seen.

The cat trotted ahead of him down the hallway. He peered through the open doors of his room and saw nothing. Marmy continued to the end of the hallway.

The shooter was on the stairs.

Luke pushed open Jillian's door. The room was empty. "Jillian?" he whispered.

The cat moved toward the closet and Jillian stepped out.

He put his finger to his lips, closed the bedroom door and locked it before leading her into the bathroom and shutting and locking that door as well. The shooter would search his room and maybe his mother's before coming to the end of the hall.

That and the time it would take to break down the doors bought them only precious minutes. Luke flung open the window and grabbed a towel.

The banging on the bedroom door had begun by the time Jillian had crawled through the window and slid to the end of the towel before dropping to the ground.

He had crawled out and hung from the windowsill looking for trim that might provide a foothold when the banging abruptly stopped.

A second later, the wail of sirens reached Luke's ears. He dropped to the ground, landing hard but on his feet. Jillian reached for his hand.

When they hurried around to the front of the house, Angie had already gotten out of her patrol car with her gun drawn, and Chris's patrol car was coming up the road.

Luke glanced all around the property, speculating on which way the shooter would have gone. There were a thousand places to hide. His best guess was that he'd sought a route of escape when he heard the sirens. There was no sign of where the man had concealed his car.

Angie hurried toward him as she continued to survey the area with her weapon ready.

"You didn't see a car parked anywhere on the way in?" Luke asked.

She shook her head.

Chris came to a stop and got out of his patrol car as well. He'd grabbed his rifle from the back of the vehicle.

The shooter had to be parked somewhere.

"I'll search the road," Angie said and headed back to her patrol car.

Luke turned toward Jillian. "Get in Chris's patrol car, down out of sight, lock the doors and stay there."

Chris approached Luke. They had originally seen the shooter on the hill across the road. Maybe he'd parked his car on the other side of the hill on some little dirt track.

Luke scanned the hill but didn't see any sign of the shooter. He spoke to Chris. "Head up that way. I need to get my firearm and some ammo."

By the time Luke had grabbed a box of bullets from his truck and retrieved his rifle, Jillian was safe inside the patrol car, and Chris was halfway up the hill. He crossed the road and headed up the slope as well. Chris and Angie were in uniform and would be able to communicate via radio. He turned to look back at the farm.

Jillian was hidden in the passenger seat of the

patrol car. They didn't know for sure where the attacker had gone, but he could be lurking nearby, waiting to get to Jillian.

Luke went to the top of the hill but couldn't see Chris. He must've kept moving. He pulled his phone and dialed the deputy.

"Anything?"

Chris responded, "No sign of him. I can see a flat open spot down below where someone could have parked a car."

"If that's the case, he's got to come out somewhere. Maybe Angie will spot him. I'm going to hang closer to the farm, keep Jillian in view just in case he's still on the property."

"What's going on anyway? I thought our guy was in custody."

He had to keep Jillian's secret. "I'm not sure. Let me know if Angie sees anything."

"Got it." Chris's crisp voice came through the phone.

Luke walked the hill parallel to the road, searching the clusters of trees and the high grass, ready to fire the rifle if he had to. He watched the cornfield and the outbuildings as well for any sign of movement. If the guy had stayed behind and was going to try another shot, he would've taken it by now. He must've chosen to get away. That didn't mean he wouldn't look for another chance to get at Jillian. It wasn't safe for her here. She had to get out.

Luke moved back down the hill toward the patrol car. As he drew close, Jillian got out of the car and hurried toward him. The glow of affection on her face reminded him of the kiss that they'd shared.

Everything was different now. Jillian would be leaving. Once again, the life he thought he might have had been ripped away from him.

"I think you have a phone call to make to Marshal Stiller." He lifted an arm to embrace her, but he let it fall at his side.

Her smile faded and she stopped short of falling against him. "Yes, I better do that. It's time to leave town once and for all."

THIRTEEN

Jillian sat in the bedroom staring at her phone as sadness and frustration settled around her. Marmy snuggled in beside her. Downstairs she could hear Luke making arrangements to get the broken window fixed, and then it sounded like he was talking to one of his deputies.

His sudden distance toward her wasn't a surprise. He'd barely looked her way as they walked back to the house. She wasn't going to be in this town much longer. She understood, but it still hurt.

She could feel her body going numb as she called Marshal Stiller. After four rings, the phone went to voice mail. She took in a breath before speaking. "Marshal Stiller. It's Jillian. I need to get out of Spring Meadow for good. Long story. Bottom line, I'm not safe here." It felt as though a tight cord had been wrapped around her chest. "They found me." She clicked the disconnect button and closed her eyes.

Luke's warm voice floated toward her. "He's not there?"

She shook her head. "I'm sure he'll call back as soon as he can."

"My deputies are starting to wonder what's going on."

Did it even matter at this point if they knew? She'd be in a whole different location soon. Still, the more people who knew who she really was meant the trail of where she would end up would be that much easier to follow. They found her once, they might find her again.

She opened her eyes. Luke was so tall he nearly filled the doorway. "What did you tell them?" she said.

"That I didn't know what was going on. I sent them back into town."

"Do you think that man with the rifle is still around here?"

Luke shrugged. "I'm not sure. We can't take any chances. We need to get you out of here. Even if it's just temporary until we hear from the marshal. Mom will be back soon. I'm going to have to warn her about the damage to the house."

Luke and his family had paid a high price for her to be here. She was tired of being a burden to him and those he cared about. "I'm so sorry about all of this."

Tears rimmed her eyes again. She thought of

the little house she had lived in for three years. The treasures she'd collected. The furniture she'd bought. The books she loved. Though she had to be guarded around neighbors and friends, she had come to care about them. She'd have to walk away from all of it again. "Please, say I can at least come back and get the cats." She brushed her hand over Marmy's soft fur.

The dullness in his eyes and his flat tone suggested sadness. "Maybe we can figure out some way to deliver them to you."

She stepped toward him. "Before we go, let me at least look at the wound on your shoulder."

He tugged on his sleeve. "It just stings, is all."

"Let me examine it." Her voice was more forceful this time.

"Yes, nurse Jillian." The lightness of his tone and the smile that graced his face was like a soothing balm to her.

"Been a long time since I've been called 'nurse.'" She couldn't purge the grief from her words.

After sitting down on the bed, Luke took off his blue jacket and lifted the sleeve of his T-shirt. The bullet had caused bleeding and a tear. She touched the area around the cut.

Luke squinted like he was trying to hide his pain.

"It does hurt, doesn't it?"

"A little."

Both their heads were turned toward his shoulder, and she could hear him breathing. His proximity made her feel lightheaded. She looked into his eyes. "We should probably at least put some disinfectant on it and cover it. I think I saw a first aid kit in the bathroom."

She retreated to get it, and when she returned, he was sitting on the bed with the ginger cat nesting close to his thigh. Jillian dressed the wound and placed gauze and tape over it.

"Thank you." He rose to his feet. "We shouldn't take any more time. Let's get in my truck. I need to grab a different coat."

"Where are we going?"

"I don't know. I just don't think it's wise to stay here."

Minutes later, after saying goodbye to her cats, she sat in the cab of Luke's old truck. She'd packed the clothes and toiletries she'd brought with her and put the duffle in the truck bed. "Will your mom be back soon enough to take care of the cats?"

"I already texted Matt and let him know to feed them."

Luke returned his rifle to the rack and placed the box of ammo in the glove compartment. As he got behind the steering wheel, his open denim jacket revealed that he wore a shoulder holster. He was expecting more trouble.

The hole where the bullet had gone through the passenger window was a reminder of what they were dealing with.

"This kind of goes beyond your duties as a sheriff," she commented.

He shook his head. "No, not really. The marshal expects me to protect you if there is a threat until I can hand you off to him."

The cold official tone of his voice made her sad. She wanted to talk about the kiss and what it meant. She stared at the house. Luke had taped over the broken window. Gray clouds indicated that rain was on the way. "I wish I could stay here in Spring Meadow."

"I wish that too." His voice faltered, but then he lifted his chin and his jaw grew tight. "Nothing is permanent in this world."

"Nothing but God's love and his faithfulness," she said.

"True. It's hard to lose everything though." Luke's eyes glazed and he looked away.

He of all people understood. Her throat went tight over the pain he'd experienced in his life.

Luke pulled out onto the country road. Neither of them spoke until he came to the paved street and turned in the direction that would lead them away from town.

"What's the plan here?" she asked. "Just to drive around?"

"I'm hoping the marshal calls back soon and can set up a safe place for me to take you." He glanced in his rearview mirror. "Until then, let's just make sure we're not followed."

As he drove and the traffic got heavier, she found herself checking the side mirror. There were several cars behind them. After ten miles, a sign on the road told them they were five miles from the next town, called Nowhere.

"Are you hungry?"

"Starving," she said.

"There's a place up here that has really good fried chicken."

Luke took the only exit into town. Main Street of Nowhere had no stop lights and looked to be only a couple of blocks long. Years ago, she'd driven out here to an estate sale when she was trying to furnish her house. She couldn't believe it was a real place.

The café had a broken neon sign that said they were open. The *e* in the word *open* no longer worked.

Luke parked his truck next to a small car. "We'll get it to go. There's no reason for us to stay out in public."

Luke was operating under the assumption that she was still in danger. That was probably smart.

She still couldn't fathom how the mafia had found her after all these years. It was hard enough to deal with what had happened with Roger.

They stepped inside and placed their order at the counter. Most of the tables were full. The place buzzed with conversation, laughter and the clatter of silverware. This was probably the only restaurant in town to eat at. Anyone here would know they were from out of town. Someone would remember seeing them if questioned by the man who was after her. Though Luke had changed out of his bloody jacket for a denim one, they both looked like they'd been dragged behind a truck because they hadn't had a chance to change since leaving the hospital. Yet another reason why they would be memorable.

Their order was delivered within a few minutes. The spices on the chicken wafted up to her nose as she held the to-go containers and headed back out to the truck. When they stepped outside, rain sprinkled down on them.

Two other cars had pulled up in the time that they'd been inside. Both were empty and there was a truck across the street. The slant of the light didn't allow her to see the driver behind the wheel, which made her nervous.

Luke kept his eyes on them for a moment before opening his door. "I kind of wish my old truck wasn't so distinctive." He slipped lower behind the wheel.

Once she was settled in the passenger seat, she asked, "Why do you keep such an old truck anyway?"

Luke stared down at his closed to-go container. "It was the last truck my father drove before he died."

A relic of the past that he held on to. She'd been whisked away from her apartment in New Jersey so quickly that there had only been time to grab two photos from a shelf by the door, a picture with her father taken shortly before he died. Her mother had died when she was a teenager, and she was an only child. The other photo was of her with the rest of the ER staff at a Christmas party. She kept the photos hidden, rarely taking them out to look at them.

Luke drove to the edge of town, stopping by a park. The leaves in the tall trees were beautiful shades of gold and red. A few children played in the puddles while their mothers watched close by, holding umbrellas.

Droplets of water splattered against the windshield.

She dug her plastic fork into her coleslaw after consuming a chicken leg. "How does a little town like this survive?"

"They used to have a stock sale here once a

month. I always went with my dad. I think the grain elevators are still operational."

She tried to picture Luke as a boy riding with his father in a truck to buy cows. "You liked working on the farm?"

"It was part of my upbringing. Part of who I am, I guess."

"Matt says it's not profitable anymore," she hedged.

Luke shrugged. "We break even. I have some more ideas for ways to make money, but Matt and Mom aren't interested."

"Lot of extra labor for everyone. It seems that their priority is not with the farm anymore."

He shook his head, then grinned. "You've been talking to my family. I know that both my mom and Matt want to sell the remaining acres. They no longer feel a connection to the land." He set his bare chicken leg back in the box and dug into his mashed potatoes.

"What makes you want to keep it?"

He shrugged again and finished off the rest of his potatoes. He closed the to-go container and stared through the windshield. "I don't know. Guess because it's a piece of my childhood. I don't mean to be stubborn. I just wish Mom and Matt could catch a vision for what we could do with the farm."

The quality of his voice had changed, become

more intense. She knew she was treading on delicate emotional territory. "Maybe there's a different reason you hold on, and they're ready to let go."

"What do you mean?"

Before the day was over, they would probably be saying goodbye and never see each other again. He had helped her, protected her. She wanted to do something for him. "Didn't you say that you and your fiancée had made plans to run the farm together since Matt wasn't interested even back then?"

Luke's eyebrows furrowed and his lips drew into a tight line. "I hadn't thought of it that way. But maybe it is the last piece of her. The last piece of the dream." His Adam's apple moved up and down and his voice faltered. "Maybe that is why I'm holding on."

She reached over and touched his arm. "I know it's hard to let go of the past and start over."

"But that's what you had to do." When he looked at her, his eyes were vulnerable. "Guess I've been stuck for a long time." He shook his head. "Maybe it's time to get unstuck." He set the to-go container aside and turned the key in the ignition.

His action signaled that the conversation was over, but it was clear from the faraway look in his eyes and the silence that followed that he was still thinking about what she'd said. He drove up the quiet streets of Nowhere. Her phone buzzed. A text from Marshal Stiller.

Busy. In the middle of a transport. Will get back to you as soon as I can.

She read the message out loud, adding, "I hope he can contact me soon. I'm sure your deputies need you back on the job."

"They'll be okay in the short term. Angie could run that place if she wanted to."

"The sheriff's department doesn't have anything like a safe house, do they?"

"Not officially. No. That's not something we have the finances for."

"But there might be a place?"

He nodded, appearing pensive. "I have a friend, Tom, who owns a fishing lodge. We kept a domestic violence case there, a mom and her two kids, until her folks could come get her. Things were so bad she wasn't even safe at the shelter, and we didn't want to endanger the other women."

"Maybe we could stay there while we wait to hear from Marshal Stiller," said Jillian.

He nodded but didn't say anything further. Silence threaded through the truck as Luke pulled back out onto the highway.

She stared down at the two empty to-go containers on the console between them. "I'm going to miss you, Luke."

He kept his hands on the wheel and stared out the window. They passed another sign. The next town was twenty miles away. How far was the fishing lodge?

"I'm going to miss you too, but that's just how it goes, right?" The icy tone had come back into his voice, making it clear he wasn't going to let himself be vulnerable again. "People leave. Life goes on."

She wasn't sure what to say. He had put up a wall. The car rolled down the highway. The broken yellow lines flicked by, and the trees that lined the road blurred. She didn't want to part with Luke on these terms. Was there something more she could say?

His gaze went from the side view mirror to the rearview. "That guy has been behind us for a long time." She glanced over her shoulder out the back window, wondering what had alarmed him. A large truck loomed toward them. Suddenly it sped up, closing the distance between them and hitting their back bumper.

The first tap caused her to jerk in her seat. Her heart beat faster as Luke pressed the gas. The second hit came more violently, making her whole body shake as she reached out to brace her hand on the dashboard.

The truck meant to run them off the road.

Through the smear of the rain coming down, the headlights of the other truck shone. Luke had been ruminating over the conversation with Jillian and lost his focus on watching the road for only a few minutes. It had been enough time for the other truck to zoom up and ambush them.

His old truck burst ahead only briefly before the larger, newer one caught up with them. This time the truck turned into the oncoming lane before the driver slammed into the bed of Luke's truck two times.

Luke's backend swung out kicking up the gravel on the side of the road.

He angled the steering wheel straightening the tire so he could press the accelerator to the floor.

The larger truck got almost even with them and rammed against him. This time his truck went completely off the road into the gravel.

His truck moved in a serpentine pattern as the other vehicle hit them once more on the back bumper.

Jillian screamed.

A tree loomed in front of them. Luke pumped the brakes and turned the wheel to avoid hitting the tree head on. All the same, the tree impacted with the edge of the hood causing it to crumple. Steam rolled out of the engine. The other truck was slowing down, preparing to come to a stop behind them.

"Get out."

Jillian had already pushed the door open. There was no time to grab his rifle. Luke opened his door and ducked just as a gunshot shattered his back window.

Adrenaline surged through his body as he ran around to the front of the truck. Rain pattered his head and shoulders. He could just make out Jillian as she scrambled up the side of the muddy hill, the cover of the trees still feet away. She was the shooter's primary target.

Luke had to stop him.

The shooter rested his rifle on the hood of his truck, lining up a shot on Jillian. She wouldn't make it to the trees in time.

Luke straightened and pulled his handgun from the shoulder holster. He advanced toward the other man, firing off a shot just as the shooter was about to pull the trigger.

Jillian stopped and looked over her shoulder but then continued up the hill drawing closer to the trees. The shooter turned his attention on Luke, lifting and aiming his rifle as Luke sought cover at the front of his truck.

A rifle shot whizzed by him just as he crouched

at the truck bumper. He kept moving with his gun drawn in the direction Jillian had gone. He had to hold this guy off.

He hurried up the hill in a zigzag pattern, turning to fire off a shot. Anything to delay the man from pulling the trigger again. The shooter ducked down behind his truck hood.

Luke scrambled up the mud-slick hill into the trees just as another shot echoed behind him.

He scanned the area but didn't see Jillian anywhere. She must've kept moving. Knowing that the shooter would follow him, he sprinted through the forest taking the most likely path that Jillian could have gone. He searched for her as he kept running, scanning the trees for any sign of her.

He ran for a few minutes before he saw her up ahead just as she disappeared into a cluster of evergreens. He didn't hear any noise behind him to indicate that the shooter had followed him. The guy was probably pretty stealthy. Luke had to assume they'd be followed.

He hurried toward where he'd last seen Jillian, pumping his legs and willing himself to go faster. She stepped out from behind a tree, and he nearly crashed into her. His arms reached out toward her.

She fell into his embrace. "Glad you made it."

The hug was brief. He tugged on the sleeve of her rain-soaked jacket. "We better keep moving."

As they ran, the trees thinned, and he surveyed the area, wondering if there was a hiding spot where he might be able to take the shooter by surprise. There had been no time to call his deputies to see if they could alert highway patrol. When he peered over his shoulder, he caught flashes of movement in the trees. The guy was still too close. He'd be slowed by having to carry the rifle, but they had to put some distance between them if they were to get the jump on the gunman and then make a call for help.

Jillian kept pace with him as he sprinted. The shooter emerged from the trees. His heart pounded. He pivoted, looking for cover.

They entered another cluster of lodgepole pines that would partially shield them from view. They weren't going to outrun this guy. "This way," Luke said.

He started to move parallel to the road below. His truck probably didn't run anymore, but the shooter's was still operational. If they could escape in the shooter's truck, it would be easy enough to call for backup to help search for a man while he was on foot.

Rain soaked though his coat and chilled his skin. The grove of trees that had shielded them from view ended. He dropped to the ground. The tall grass provided a degree of cover as he tried to assess where the shooter was. Jillian followed. Both rested on their stomachs on the wet grass close enough that her shoulder brushed against his.

The rain kept coming down as he peered through the grass. Drops pounded his bare head and trailed down his face.

The shooter came to an open area and glanced in one direction and then the other. Luke held his breath, watching and hoping that the blue of his jacket wouldn't give them away in the wheat-colored grass.

Go the other way.

The shooter took off up the hill.

He let out the breath he'd been holding. This was their chance to get downhill to that truck. He waited until the trees enveloped the shooter before bursting to his feet and heading straight downhill.

Jillian was right beside him, but the mud and the steepness of the hill caused her leg to slide out in front of her. She reached her hand out to brace her fall. He grabbed her arm and pulled her back up to her feet. This part of the mountain was rockier than the way they'd come up. The terrain slowed them down.

A rifle shot echoed down the mountain. They'd been spotted. The guy was good at tracking and shooting, which made Luke wonder if he'd at some training, maybe military. The intensity of the boom made his heart beat faster, but they both kept running. Right before they entered an area filled with brush and trees, he glanced in the direction the shot had come from, but he didn't see any signs of the shooter.

The guy had probably figured out their plan since he was headed down the hill as well.

Slipping and sliding, they made it nearly to the bottom of the hill before Luke stopped and crouched behind a bush.

The man pursuing them didn't have to make it all the way down to be a threat. He just had to get close enough to line up a shot. They would be exposed and out in the open once they got close to the working truck. And if the keys had not been left in the ignition, he would need a minute to hot-wire it. That too would leave them vulnerable. He made a split-second decision.

Hesitation would only make them more of a target.

"Let's go."

He burst out into the open with Jillian close behind him. They were within feet of the truck when another shot cracked the air around them.

Luke's knees buckled and he fell.

FOURTEEN

When Luke hit the ground, Jillian initially thought he'd been shot. She gasped and reached out for him. Mud smeared across his pant leg. No sign of blood. He righted himself. He'd slipped.

"Hurry, before he shoots again!" he said.

Grabbing her hand, he rushed back toward the trees, which caused them to have to veer off the straight path they'd been on to get to the truck.

He pulled her behind a tree with a large trunk. She pressed against his back as he peered out.

The sprinkling and spattering of the rain was the only sound she could hear besides her own intense breathing. "Can you see him?"

Luke shook his head causing droplets to spray off his shaggy blond hair.

The seconds ticked by.

"He's not moving. Wherever he is, he's waiting for us to step out into the open." Luke pressed against the tree trunk and pulled his phone out. He spoke in a low voice to Deputy Angie Walters, advising her of their location and commanding her to get in touch with highway patrol.

Unless highway patrol was close, they were still on their own in the short term. He put his phone away.

"He's not going to let us get near that truck. My guess is he's concealed himself halfway up the hill, watching with a shot already lined up. It will only take him a second to get another one off. If we step out in the open, we're both dead."

Getting to the truck had no longer become an option. She tried to shake off the despair that realization caused.

Luke pivoted one way and then the other. He turned to face her, cupping his hand on her shoulder. "You stay put."

"What are you going to do?"

"I'm going to try to get him to take another shot. See if I can pinpoint where he's hunkered down at. I'll move in. If I can get close enough, I might be able to shoot him. If nothing else, it will force him to move."

"Luke, that's too dangerous." She put her hands on his chest. He'd be risking his life.

He gazed down at her, then touched her cheek before kissing her lightly. "It'll be all right. You stay hidden and still."

The kiss soothed her fear but left her wishing she could stay in his arms even longer.

Her heart pounded, matching the rhythm of the rain as Luke eased his body away from the tree that had provided a degree of protection. Her breath caught when he took a step out into the open.

Nothing happened. She had only a partial view of the hillside where Luke had indicated the shooter probably was.

Luke moved toward a bush and crouched. A rifle shot close to Luke echoed in the rain.

She saw now where the shooter was. A head had bobbed above some tall grass.

She stared down at the road where the two trucks were. They had been a short distance away from getting to that truck. The shooter was moving again. No doubt he was focused on getting at Luke. He'd be distracted. He couldn't watch them both. Luke didn't need to fight this battle alone; she had to find a way to help.

She angled around the side of the tree and burst out, running toward the truck down the rocky hillside. She nearly slammed into the passenger side from the momentum of the downhill run. She sprinted around to the driver's side and yanked open the door. No keys, and she didn't know how to hot-wire a car.

She stared above the edge of the truck bed as her heart pounded. When she glanced up the hillside, she couldn't see Luke or the shooter.

Luke must have seen where she'd gone, but maybe the shooter hadn't. Otherwise, it seemed like he would have taken a shot at her before she got to the secure side of the truck.

She continued to stare at the hillside as the rain came down. She caught a glimpse of blue in the gold and red of a bush. Luke's denim jacket. Luke had moved closer to where the shooter had last been spotted.

Her phone rang. Marshal Stiller. She feared the noise would draw attention to her. She hit the disconnect button and crouched low. Luke's truck wasn't that far away. She ran toward it. Though the whole front end of the truck was bent, and the hood had crumpled when it hit the tree, she could still get the driver's side door open.

Her breathing had become erratic as she reached in and grabbed the rifle and then crawled across the seat to pull the ammo out of the glove compartment. She had shot a rifle only a few times in her life when her grandfather had taken her to the range as a teen.

Her hand was shaking as she lifted a long bullet from the box, pulled the bolt back and placed it in the internal magazine. She put in three more bullets.

The click of the truck door shutting seemed to echo in the downpour of rain. Before she could even rest the barrel of the rifle on the truck bed, another gunshot shattered the silence.

That shot had come from a pistol. Her gaze darted back and forth up and down the hillside. Her eye went toward a flutter of movement. She caught a glimpse of the shooter's head and pulled the trigger. And then pulled it again.

She heard rocks crashing against each other. Luke had made it down the hillside and was headed around to the driver's side of the working truck.

A shot came from the hillside. Luke disappeared from view on the passenger side of the truck bed.

No, God, don't let him be hit.

His head bobbed up a second later, then he came around to the front side of the truck. He swung open the driver's side door, signaling for her to come toward him. She still held the rifle as she got into the cab of the truck and scooted over to the passenger side, staying low and out of view.

Luke jumped in, sliding down low in the seat as well while he pulled wires from beneath the dash. The engine started up a second later. The first shot was fired before Luke could even shift into Drive. It must have hit the truck bed. Another shot came right after that. She wasn't sure where that one had gone.

The shooter was heading down the hill.

Luke pressed the accelerator and pulled out. The truck rolled onto the paved road. Jillian watched just above the edge of the window as the shooter stood out in the open, lining up another shot. She considered firing back with the rifle she still held but doubted she could make the shot. She saw him clearly. There was something familiar about him. She cringed. Fearing she'd be caught in a spray of broken glass, she braced when the recoiling rifle butt hit the sniper's padded shoulder. She heard only a pinging noise that indicated the bullet had hit something.

Luke sped up. It took only a few minutes to realize where the rifle shots had gone. The truck lurched, chugged and wobbled. Luke pulled off on a shoulder and the engine quit.

He tapped the wires together, but the truck made only a huffing noise before dying all together.

They locked eyes for only a moment. It was just a matter of minutes before the shooter made it down to the road. He'd made sure they couldn't escape in the truck.

They were on the run again.

Luke pushed his door open as Jillian got out of the passenger side. She met him on his side of the vehicle that was closer to the trees. Rain still spilled from the sky, causing him to shiver.

"Stay by the front bumper." He took the rifle from her. He scanned the hillside by the road. Then he lifted the rifle to peer through the scope but still didn't see anything. They couldn't stay here. He had to assume the guy was going to come after them, hunt them down.

They were both cold and soaked to the bone.

He saw movement by his old truck. The sniper was already down by the road.

He'd noticed a few cars going by when he'd been hunkered down on the hillside. To stop a driver, though, would mean putting them in danger too.

Jillian lifted her head above the hood of the truck. He backed toward her, still watching the road, prepared to fire the rifle. The guy was being careful not to come out into the open.

Luke backed up toward Jillian without taking his eyes off where he'd last seen the sniper. She touched the back of his arm.

He turned his head slightly and whispered, "Toward the trees. I'm right behind you."

Highway patrol must be close by now. He needed a few precious minutes to call his deputy so Angie could radio the highway patrol of their exact location.

When he glanced over his shoulder, he saw Jillian disappear into the trees. He backed away from the defunct truck, still hoping to catch sight of the sniper. Carrying the rifle would slow him down, but he held on to it for now.

He caught up with Jillian, and together they ran deeper into the trees. He directed her toward some thick brush that would provide a hiding spot. They knelt facing each other. Rain trickled off Jillian's hair. She crossed her arms over her body and shivered.

He pressed the button to reach Angie. "Highway patrol should be close by now, Luke," she said by way of greeting. The sound of her confident voice eased the tension in his body.

He replied in a low voice, not wanting to risk the shooter being close enough to hear him. "If you can radio highway patrol. The sniper is still in the area and might try to take them out."

"I'll let them know the risk level. Maybe they can call in some backup."

"We're hiding in the trees on the east side of the road just a ways north of mile marker thirty-two. I'll try to get us to a place where we have a view of the highway."

"Ten-four. Take care."

They wove through the forest until he heard several cars go by on the road. He spotted a cluster of trees not too far from the road that would conceal them. Jillian pressed in close to him as he peered out from behind a tree, lifting the rifle and watching.

He heard sirens in the distance. Highway patrol was announcing their arrival, maybe to scare off the sniper.

He continued to watch the road.

A white SUV rolled by and came to a stop not too far from his truck. The sniper ran out and jumped in the passenger seat. The SUV sped up.

"What's going on?" Jillian spoke behind him.

Luke turned his head sideways. "He's got help." The sniper must have realized he'd be caught if he stayed on foot once he'd made his own truck inoperable. The call had to have been made even before highway patrol announced their arrival.

The highway patrol vehicle came from the direction the white SUV had gone. A second later, another highway patrol car coming in the opposite direction became visible.

Luke ran out on the road to stop the highway patrol officer. A fortysomething woman rolled down the window and stuck her head out.

Luke pointed in the direction the vehicle had gone. "Our guy got away in a white SUV." He'd been too far away to make note of the license plate number.

"I'll see if I can catch him." The highway patrol officer nodded and started moving even before the window was rolled up.

The other officer brought his vehicle to a stop not too far from where they were. Jillian ran out from the hiding place. Luke took her hand, and they hurried toward the patrol car.

They both got in the back of the vehicle.

The officer, a younger man with a buzz cut, glanced back at them. "There's a blanket underneath the seat. Looks like I need to get you two to a hospital."

"Just some place where we can get warmed up." The nearest hospital was in Spring Meadow. He didn't want to take Jillian back there. The shooter was mobile now and might conclude that they would go there.

Luke grabbed the blanket. After unfolding it and placing it on his back, he wrapped his arm around Jillian so they both would be covered. Jillian's body seemed to vibrate from shivering as he drew her closer.

"Any ideas where that might be?" The young officer watched them in the rearview mirror.

His friend's fishing lodge wasn't far from here. Luke gave the officer directions and an address so he could punch it into his GPS.

Jillian's voice trembled from how chilled she was. "Marshal Stiller called back," she murmured. "I wasn't able to talk to him."

They couldn't do the phone call with the patrol officer listening. "Text him back," Luke whispered. "See if he has a place set up for you." If

Marshal Stiller had a safe house available, they could go straight there.

"I will." She pulled the blanket tighter around her shoulders. "I just need to get warmed up a little."

"Do you think you could identify the man who came after us?"

She nodded. "I did see him when he stepped out into the open. He kind of looked like the guy I put in jail… Gordon Burnett. I wonder if they're related."

"I saw him too," said Luke.

After Jillian's shivering subsided, she pulled her phone out and pressed buttons to text the marshal.

Luke listened to the radio exchange between the two patrol officers. The female officer had spotted the white SUV, but it had taken an abrupt turn in the middle of the road when it realized it was being followed.

The female officer's voice came through the radio. "I'm getting turned around now. I no longer have visual on him. He's headed in your direction unless he turns off somewhere."

Jillian tensed next to him and stopped texting. "He's coming back this way?"

They were dealing with two men now. Would they be bold enough to come after Jillian while she was in the patrol car? A marked highway patrol car would be easy enough to spot and keep track of and that was concerning.

"Will keep an eye out," said the younger officer.

"I'll stay in pursuit for now," responded the female officer.

Jillian pressed a button on her phone and stared at it. She spoke up after a few minutes. "There aren't any available safe houses close by. He's still trying to set something up."

Luke called his friend Tom at the fishing lodge to let him know they would be coming. He checked the cars behind him, a large blue truck and another smaller car he couldn't fully see because the truck blocked it on the road.

The female officer radioed that she had to deal with another call, a stranded driver stuck on a muddy side road.

Traffic grew heavier as they got closer to a town. The highway patrol officer turned off the main road onto one that led to the lodge.

The rain had turned to a drizzle as they headed up the gravel road. The lodge came into view. Tom stood on the covered porch with his hands crossed over his chest. A welcome sight. He was a tall lean red-headed man who was fond of wearing plaid shirts.

Luke thanked the officer and ushered Jillian up the steps to the protection of the cabin. He had a lot of problems to solve. They needed to have a private conversation with the marshal. If he couldn't arrange for Jillian's transport from the lodge once a safe house was set up, Luke would have to come up with something.

He needed to get back to his duties as the sheriff, but he wouldn't leave Jillian until he could ensure her safety. Duty wasn't the only thing that made him want to stay. He cared about her even if she wouldn't be in his life much longer.

Tom offered Luke a hardy slap on the back. "Good to see you, man."

Luke hadn't explained much in his call—only that he and a friend needed a place to hole up for a while. "This is Jillian."

Tom nodded and held out a hand toward her. "Nice to meet you. You both look like something the cat dragged in. Why don't you come in and get comfortable?"

He appreciated that Tom wasn't demanding an explanation for why they looked the way they did.

His friend stepped aside so Jillian could go in first.

Before following, Luke glanced up the road that led to the lodge. The backend of the highway patrol vehicle was still visible. This road came to a dead end at the lake. There were no other residences out here. If the sniper had seen where they turned, he would know where they were.

FIFTEEN

Inside the main room of the lodge, a fire was burning. The place was toasty warm. Leather sofas and chairs formed a half circle around the fireplace. Through the floor-to-ceiling windows, a lake surrounded by forest was visible with four motorboats secured at the dock.

"Why don't you two get warmed up? I've got some hot cider going in the kitchen." Tom disappeared behind a door.

Jillian sat down on one end of the couch, and Luke took a seat in a chair close to fire. The heat and crackling of the fire provided calming comfort. Though they'd warmed up some in the patrol car, they were both still muddy and soaking wet.

Tom returned and handed them both steaming mugs. "You both look like you could use a shower and some clean clothes."

Jillian took a sip of her cider and let the sweetness and warmth coat her tongue.

Luke pulled his soaked shirt away from his body. "That would be good."

Tom looked at Luke. "I can loan you some of my clothes and, Jillian, I'll see what I can rustle up for you from the clothes that have been left behind by guests."

"Thanks, Tom," Luke said.

His friend left the room again. Luke and Jillian stared at the fire for a long moment. Exhaustion settled into her bones.

She could hear Tom's footsteps coming back up the hallway.

"We need to call the marshal when we can get a private moment," Luke said.

She nodded.

Tom set two piles of clothes on the side table by the couch. "There you go. Luke, you can use my shower. Jillian the black bear room is open to you. If you don't mind, I have a group coming in a few days, and I still need to get a few things done."

Jillian nodded. "Thanks for everything, Tom."

Tom glanced at her. "Luke knows where the washer and dryer are. You can toss your muddy clothes in. Help yourself to the food in the kitchen." Tom left the room and went out the door that led to the lake.

Jillian finished her cider and took the pile of women's clothes. Luke pointed her in the direction she needed to go, and then he went down the opposite hallway. She passed a door with a picture of a moose on it and another that featured a bald eagle. The next door featured a picture of a black bear.

She stepped inside. She was worn out, and her muscles ached from all the running she'd done. She freshened up and got settled, all while tears flowed down her cheeks.

This had all been too much.

She found herself longing for the comfort and safety of Luke's arms. He'd kissed her a second time when they'd been in so much danger.

She had to let go of the idea that there could be anything between them. If she wasn't killed first, she'd be stepping into a new life without him.

She dressed and found a comb to run through her hair. When she came back into the great room, Luke was looking fresh and clean too. His blond hair was wet and slicked back off his face.

Through the large windows that faced the lake, she could see Tom carrying some lawn chairs toward a firepit. It had stopped raining.

She held her phone up. "Let's make that call to Marshal Stiller."

She sat close to him on the sofa and pressed the call button. Marshal Stiller answered right away. She put the phone on speaker so Luke could hear.

"Jillian. You're safe," the marshal said.

She glanced at Luke. "Relatively." She told him about the attack from the sniper. "And now he's got another guy with him."

"Clearly, we need to get you out of there and work on figuring out who this guy is," Stiller said.

"Yes, I need to leave this area." Her throat had gone dry. "I think I could identify him from a database. He looked like Gordon Burnett."

There was silence on the line, as if the marshal was processing that news. "If I remember correctly, Gordon Burnett had a brother," Stiller said.

She and Luke were both bent close to the phone where she'd set it on the coffee table.

Marshal Stiller's voice came back online. "I'm on my way to Spring Meadow. I can place you short term in a safe house about a hundred miles from there." Luke sat up straight and ran his hands through his hair. When she turned to look into his eyes, she thought she saw hurt in his expression.

This was how it had to be. They both knew that.

"I'm not in Spring Meadow anymore." She gave him the location of the fishing lodge.

"Let me punch it into the GPS. Give me a second." The line went silent for a minute. "Okay, I see where you are. It'll be after dark by the time I get there, but I don't think we should delay this.

Let's get you out of there. We have to assume that as long as you are in the area, you're not safe."

"That's a solid assessment," said Luke.

"I'll get there as fast as I can," said the marshal.

They said their goodbyes, and Jillian disconnected.

She sat back on the couch. "Looks like we'll just have to wait here."

Luke rose to his feet. The shoulder holster with the handgun was visible under the open flannel shirt he wore. He also had a T-shirt on.

She rose and walked toward him. "I guess after tonight, we'll be saying goodbye." There was so much more she wanted to tell him. "If I don't get a chance to say it, thank you for everything."

"Sounds like you might be at the safe house for a few days at least. I'll try to figure out a way to get the cats to you."

She was leaving behind so much that she was going to miss, but to have the cats would have to be enough. "All these things we cling to, huh? When the only real constant in any life is God and His faithfulness."

"I know. You said that before. I've been thinking about what you said about the farm. Why I don't want to sell when it would be the best thing for everyone. I guess it really was the final piece I had left of Maria and the plans we made together."

"That's a big step, Luke."

"I've been living in the past thinking I could get it back by holding onto the land. In the process, I kept my family back from their dreams."

"It's hard to let go of things that connected us to people we loved," she said.

"But people are what matter, right?"

"Yes." Jillian looked him in the eye. "It will be good, Luke. To move forward. Not easy, but good."

"You're a wise woman." He reached up and brushed his knuckles over her cheek.

His touch sent a wave of warmth through her, but she stepped back. Much as she wanted to lean into his comfort, she couldn't cling to him when her world was changing yet again. She had to move forward too. "I'm exhausted. I'm going to get a nap."

His eyes lit up for a moment, making the gold flecks more prominent. "I'll keep watch."

She shoved her hands into the pockets of the zip-up hoodie she was wearing. They wouldn't talk about the kiss and all these feelings of affection swirling through her. After tonight, they wouldn't see each other ever again. Why prolong this? Though she wanted more than anything to fall into his arms and be held by him one more time, she offered him a weak wave and headed down the hallway to sleep.

* * *

Luke walked the perimeter of the house and watched the road as the sky grew dark and an empty feeling invaded his heart. At Tom's suggestion, he chopped some firewood. The chopping block gave him a view of the road, and it felt good to throw his restlessness into physical activity.

He didn't want to part ways with Jillian. In the short time he'd gotten to know her, he'd felt an affinity toward her that he hadn't experienced since Maria. He admired the way she wanted to help and take care of everyone and everything. But was it more than admiration? What had those kisses been about? The first one had been because at that moment, he'd thought she was going to be able to stay in Spring Meadow. He'd felt his heart opening to the possibility of something romantic between them.

And the second kiss. He had desperately wanted to comfort her and make her feel safe. Bad move on his part. Probably sent her mixed messages.

He sliced his ax through another log and tossed the two pieces on the woodpile. He pulled another log from the uncut pile and repeated the action until he was out of breath. The sky had grown black and twinkled with stars.

He collapsed on a stump. He sat for a long

time listening to the waves on the lake hitting the shore and the wind rustling tree branches.

When his breathing returned to normal, he pulled his phone out and dialed his brother's number.

"Hey, Luke. Where have you been?"

Hearing Matt's voice made his chest tight. "Dealing with some work stuff."

"You're calling kind of late. We saw the broken window at your place. I got the text about feeding the cats. Has something bad happened? Is Jillian okay?"

"Jillian's here with me. Someone did try to shoot her when she was at the farm," said Luke. "I'm sorry about the damage."

"Luke, what is going on. You sound…different."

"I just needed to talk to you and didn't want to put it off any longer."

"Okay…sure. Go ahead," said Matt.

"I owe you and Mom an apology."

"What are you talking about?"

"It makes the most sense for everyone for us to sell what remains of the farm. I'm sorry I was so stubborn."

Matt let out a breath. "Wow. Thanks for that. It was great to grow up here, but I think we all need to move on."

"Yeah, I couldn't let go because it was the last

piece of Dad…" his heart squeezed tight as his voice faltered "…and the dream Maria and I had together. Staying there won't bring dad or Maria back."

Matt didn't answer right away. "I understand why it was hard for you to let go." His voice was soft. "You've been through a lot, little brother."

The tenderness in his brother's voice was like a balm to him.

After a long silence, Matt spoke up. "I'll let Tasha and Mom know. We'll figure out the details in the next few days."

"I think we can work something out to board Princess there after it sells. She doesn't have many more years left." A lump formed in Luke's throat.

"This will all turn out okay in the end for everyone. Who knows what God has in store for you," Matt said gently. "This is a big step."

"I should be home soon. We'll take it from there." Luke hung up after saying goodbye.

He put the phone back in his pocket, rested his head in his hands and did what he had not been able to do for ten years. He wept.

SIXTEEN

Jillian awoke in darkness, surprised at how deeply she'd slept. When she checked the bedside clock, two hours had passed since she'd closed her eyes. It seemed like Marshal Stiller should be close by now, but when she checked her phone, there were no texts from him. The unmarked turnoff might be hard to see in the dark. Still, it seemed like he would have called if he was lost.

She sat up. Her stomach was growling.

She made her way up the hall and into the quiet living room, where a single lamp had been left on. Luke wasn't sitting on the couch. When she entered the kitchen, she didn't find him there either. He must be patrolling outside.

The quiet was disconcerting.

She opened the refrigerator and pulled out some cheese, meat and mustard. After making a sandwich, she ate it standing at the living room window in the silent darkness. As the minutes passed, she grew more concerned. She pulled her phone out. She needed to call Luke and then the marshal. She pressed in Luke's number.

His voice came through loud and strong. "I was just getting ready to call you. Tom went down to the lake to sit and think a while ago. He hasn't come back." His tone was urgent. "Maybe I missed him walking back to the house. Check his room."

Still holding the phone, she headed to the other side of the lodge and pushed open the door that revealed Tom's living quarters: a single large room with a bed, desk and couch and a door that must lead to a bathroom. It appeared empty. She called to him before stepping farther in but got no response. "He's not here."

"He must still be outside. I've got to see if I can find him," Luke replied. "I don't think he had his phone on him. Make sure the doors are locked."

Luke thought there was the potential for danger.

She hung up and hurried around the lodge. By the time she'd checked that all the doors were secure, her heart was pounding. When she peered outside at the lodge entrance, she could only see the faint outline of Tom's car. She hurried toward the large window on the other side of the great room that looked out on the lake. She saw a bobbing light that must be Luke searching for his friend with his phone light.

She stepped away from the window and prepared to call Marshal Stiller. Her phone rang. Luke.

"Something's wrong. He's been beat up."

She heard Tom's groaning in the background.

"We need to get out of here," Luke went on. "I'm bringing Tom up. Grab his keys from the nail in the kitchen and get to his car."

Jillian ran to the kitchen and spotted the hook with the keys. She shoved them into her pocket and headed toward the front door that would lead to Tom's car.

Gunfire erupted and a glass window shattered just as she approached the front door. One of the men was trying to break in. She turned and ran to escape through the back door.

Outside, a figure passed the sliding glass door and stopped looking around—a man with a handgun and night vision goggles. Her heart raced. She couldn't get out that way. The attacker moved toward where Luke and Tom must be closer to the lake. Would they have time to hide before they were spotted?

The man at the front door fired again. He was trying to shoot the door open. She was trapped inside.

Luke must have found a hiding place, or perhaps he had made it up the hill and was headed toward Tom's car. She had no way of knowing.

The front door flung open.

She hurried toward Tom's quarters to hide. After easing the door shut, she locked it, praying that the shooter would only do a cursory search of the lodge.

Her fingers were shaking as she sent her text to Luke.

Where are you? Shooter in the lodge. Other headed toward the lake. I'm trapped in Tom's quarters.

There was no time to wait for his reply. He might not be in a place where he could even answer it.

After putting her phone in her pocket, she stepped toward the door, twisted the locking mechanism and turned the knob. She pulled the door open only a few inches. The second man was coming this way down the hall.

She shut the door, locked it, raced across the room and flung open the window that faced the back of the house by the lake. The man with the handgun must be closer to the lake than the lodge by now. She didn't see him anywhere. The window was the only other way out of the room. She'd have to run around to the front to get to where the car was parked. Could she do that without being spotted by the man with the handgun?

The doorknob rattled and then she heard a

heavy thud, like someone throwing their body against it.

She had no choice.

She stuck her leg through the window, bent her upper body and pulled herself through. By the time her feet touched the ground, the banging had stopped. No sign of the man with the handgun. She ran toward the side of the house. Behind her, the sliding glass door opened. A second later a shot was fired in her direction just as she got around to the side of the house. It sounded like the shot had come from a rifle. The bullet had come close. That shooter must have night vision goggles as well.

She pumped her legs and headed toward the car. She swung the door open and slid behind the wheel while she fumbled in her pocket for the key. She placed it in the ignition but did not turn the key. The noise of the engine would alert the attacker to where she was if he was close. Now what?

She had maybe a minute before the attacker with the rifle came around and figured out where she'd gone.

She checked her phone. She had a text from the marshal.

Before she could click on it, the back door of the car was flung open. Luke, holding Tom by draping his arm over his shoulder, helped his friend get into the back seat and then hustled in after him.

She turned the key and the engine roared to life.

When she peered out the passenger side window, the man with the handgun was advancing toward their car from the opposite side of the lodge from where she had come.

She shifted into Reverse. The first shot pinged off the metal of Tom's car. She gasped but kept her hands on the wheel.

"Go!" said Luke.

Her heart pounded as she pressed the gas and turned on the headlights at the same time.

The back door of the car slammed shut. Apparently, he hadn't even had time to close it earlier. Luke was fumbling around for his seat belt.

The attacker with the handgun was running toward some trees where a white SUV was parked partially hidden by the trees. She drove toward the long driveway.

She sped up. In the rearview mirror, she saw the headlights of the white SUV come on.

Pressing the gas, she turned onto the long dirt road that led to the highway.

Tom groaned from the back seat.

Jillian pressed the accelerator to the floor and rounded a curve. She drove for several minutes. The other car's headlights were not visible. Why the delay? Had the attacker stopped to pick up the man with the rifle?

A tightness threaded through her torso and made her lungs feel like they were in a vise. She pressed the gas again. The car swerved on the gravel road, but she maintained her speed.

A car off the side of the road turned at an odd angle came into view. Her breath caught when her headlights illuminated the US Marshal insignia.

Had Marshal Stiller been shot? Had he been run off the road? Was he even in the car?

Luke spoke from the back seat. "Stop. I'll hold off the guy in the car so you can help the marshal."

She let up on the gas, then pressed the brake. Luke jumped out and was eaten up by the darkness as he headed back up the road. She parked her car off the road and partway down the ditch so the marshal's car would hide hers from view.

She killed the headlights.

When she glanced in the back seat, Tom looked like he was barely conscious. There was blood on his cheek. He was in no condition to help.

She jumped out of the car. The headlights of the white SUV came into view as she scrambled toward the marshal's dark vehicle. Luke had headed into the trees by the road.

Just as she got to the driver's side door, she heard the sound of gunshots.

* * *

Hidden in the trees, Luke fired twice at the white SUV as it came around the curve. One shot hit a tire and deflated it. He couldn't pinpoint where his other shot had gone. He fired a third shot.

As he sought cover, he could hear the hum of the engine stop and a car door slamming. His shots might have disabled the car. He ran deeper into the trees, scanning the darkness. The other guy had the advantage on him because of the night vision goggles.

He moved back toward where he'd left Jillian. He had to find a way to take this guy out first, though, to ensure her safety. He pressed against a tree trunk and listened. The footsteps were far apart and almost indiscernible from the other sounds of the night.

His heart hammered in his chest as he pressed his back against the tree trunk. A twig snapped, indicating that the man was within feet of Luke's hiding place. Luke held his breath and raised his gun. The man stepped in front of him. Luke hit him hard on the back of the head with the butt of the gun and the man crumpled to the ground. The guy continued to writhe.

Luke hit him again. This time, he stilled. The goggles had slipped from the man's head partway. Luke reached down, grabbed them and placed them on his own head, then pocketed the man's handgun.

Now that he could see better, he was able to move at a faster pace. Luke pushed through the trees and back up the road. He sprinted, willing his legs to work harder.

He hurried around to the marshal's car. The driver's side door was open. He touched the steering wheel where it looked slick. A coppery smell rose up as he put his fingers close to his nose. Blood.

He stalked the few feet to Tom's car, opened the passenger side door and peered inside. Tom was still in the back seat. Still conscience but bent over and listless.

Tom lifted his head. "She went looking for him."

Had the badly injured marshal feared for his life and decided to hide? Luke turned and glanced toward the trees. Or were his injuries minor, and he had decided to come to the house to protect Jillian from the oncoming assault?

He couldn't risk calling her. The assailant with the rifle was still out there. If he was close to where Jillian was, the noise would alert him to her location.

He typed a quick text to her.

Where r u? Marshal?

Noise in the trees caused him to look up. The man he'd taken the goggles and gun from had recovered and was making his way toward them. Luke ran around to the driver's side of Tom's car and got in. He handed the phone back to Tom.

"Let me know when she responds."

"Got it." Tom's voice trembled.

Luke started the car and backed out, turning the wheel so he was facing the lodge. Jillian and the marshal couldn't get far on foot. The other man emerged from the trees just as Luke gained speed.

He drove slowly, searching the trees for any sign of movement. Hopefully, Jillian would hear the car. He swerved around the white SUV. The men might have more weapons stashed in the car, but there was no time to search it.

The lodge came into view. Still no sign of Jillian or the marshal anywhere on the road or in the trees.

Tom spoke from the back seat. "She answered your text. She's inside the lodge looking for the marshal. The man with the rifle is in there too."

Jillian was in extreme danger. "Tell her we're on our way with the car," said Luke. He slowed and killed the headlights as he got closer to the lodge, fully aware that the man with the rifle might look out a window and see them.

He rolled to a stop. Though he didn't hear or

see anything, a tension hung in the air. He turned in his seat to face Tom. "How are you doing, my friend?"

Tom let out a ragged breath and pressed his hand on his stomach. "I've had better days. He beat me up pretty good. Left me alone when I faked unconsciousness. I think one of my ribs might be broken. It hurts when I breathe." He lifted the phone. "Want this?"

"Sure." Luke took the phone and typed another text, lifting his gaze between words to see if anyone was advancing toward him. The two men were probably in communication. The man he'd taken the goggles from had probably alerted the other man that the car was coming this way.

He sent the text.

Outside the lodge. Where r u?

He stared at his phone. If she didn't answer right away, it meant she was on the run and not in a secure enough place to respond…or she was under attack.

He couldn't just sit here. He had to do something. Staying out here for any length of time would make them vulnerable too. After putting his phone away, Luke pulled his gun and pushed open the door.

"I think I'll sit this one out." Tom leaned his head against the backrest.

Tom was in rough shape. "Stay low and alert."

"You got it," said Tom. He groaned as he slid down in the seat.

Luke stepped out of the car, flipped down the goggles and peered over the hood with his gun drawn. Maybe he should wait so Jillian and the marshal would know where to find them. He wrestled with his options. Staying here out in the open made them potential targets too.

His chest twisted tight. Jillian still hadn't answered the text to clue him into her location. She might be outside the lodge by now. He made his decision. He had to go find her and the marshal.

He pulled open the back door of the car. "I'm going to get them out safe. Are you strong enough to be ready to drive this thing?"

Tom sat up and nodded. "I'll be ready."

He hated leaving his friend. "You sure?"

"I can handle driving. Go." Tom waved his hand. Even in the darkness, he saw his friend wince. "Go," Tom repeated.

The longer he hesitated, the greater the potential for a bad outcome. "Take this." He handed Tom the gun he'd taken off the other man. "Keys are in the ignition." Luke ran for the cover of a bush and peered out at the front yard. How long before the man he'd disarmed made it back here? He didn't know what other weapons these men had. They could have backup guns in their vehicle.

He turned to look into the windows of the house. The great room had only a single lamp turned on. A figure that was more shadow than substance rushed by the window.

Adrenaline surged through his body as he ran the remaining distance to the front door. It looked like the door had been shot at to gain entry. He opened it and stepped inside.

SEVENTEEN

The blast from the rifle exploded around Jillian. By the time she dove for cover through the door of one of the guest rooms, she was shaking. Her heart pounded.

Hold it together, Jillian.

Footsteps in the hallway told her she didn't have much time. She clicked the lock on the door and ran across the room, pulling open a window seeking escape. The doorknob shook and then stopped. A heavy silence settled around her as a realization sank in.

The man with the rifle was going to find some other way to get to her. She could hear retreating footsteps. He'd be expecting her to come out the window like before. She ran back to the door, unlocked it and peered out.

No sign of the shooter. She heard the vague thud of a door opening. The shooter was headed toward the back side of the lodge and the window where he thought she'd come out at.

She'd been communicating with the marshal via text, which was how she learned he'd gone up to the lodge looking for her after he was run off the road. His last text said he was at the end of the hall in the laundry room. She rushed down the hall and came to the door of the laundry room. The marshal had agreed to stay put, and she would come to him. But then the man with the rifle had found her in the hallway.

When she pushed open the door, she could just make out several washers and dryers in the dark space.

"Marshal?" she whispered.

He emerged from the shadows and stepped toward her, a stocky man in his fifties graying at the temple. His right arm was curled against his body as if it was injured. There was blood on his face and a cut across his cheek. Despite his injury, the marshal had come back to the lodge trying to save her.

"Luke is out front with the car," she said.

The marshal stepped in front of her as they moved toward the side door that led outside. "Your arm, it's hurt."

"Mostly it's my hand." He held it out toward her. "I think I may have broken fingers when I braced my hand on the dashboard right before I was pushed off the road." He touched his wounded cheek. "Scraped against something sharp in the process."

While she held the underside of his hand, she leaned close and examined his fingers. Even in the dark, she could see that two of them were bent and not functional.

"We better get outside," said the marshal.

The marshal was a right-handed shooter, but he pulled his gun with his left hand. His ability to shoot accurately was seriously compromised.

"And where is our friend with the rifle?" The marshal eased the door open. "I heard the shot in the hallway."

"He went outside after that at the back of the lodge. Hard to say where he is now. He might be coming around this way to the side of the lodge," she said. "We need to hurry."

The marshal stepped out with his back against the wall, signaling for Jillian to do the same. She stepped out and pressed close to him.

They moved around the corner. The silhouette of Tom's car was in sight. Gunfire cracked the silence wide open. Several shots. The man with the rifle was shooting at Tom's car. She couldn't tell if anyone was in there. They couldn't get to the car without being shot themselves.

Jillian and the marshal stepped back and ran toward the lake side of the lodge but stopped when they heard gunfire from a single handgun. Then another handgun returned fire.

Jillian flung open the door that led back into the laundry room seeking shelter. The marshal turned so his back was to Jillian, and he could watch for anyone approaching.

Jillian ran to the laundry room window and peered above the windowsill that faced the lake, hoping to see where Luke and the other man were. She saw only shimmering water.

"Let's go." Despite whispering, Marshal Stiller's voice held an intensity.

Men with guns intending to kill her were on both sides of the lodge. Either one could come inside at any moment. There was there no safe place for them to be.

The marshal tugged on her sleeve. "We've got to try to get to that car."

The shots they'd heard by the lake meant that Luke was no longer waiting in the car. "What about Luke?"

"First the car." The marshal headed toward the door that led to the hallway past the guest rooms to the front door.

More shots came from the front side of the lodge outside. Heart pounding, she stuttered in her step but kept moving up the hallway.

Tom burst through the front door and leaned against the wall just as they entered the great room. He held a gun in his limp hand. On instinct, she and the marshal crouched by the sofa to be out of view of the big windows that faced the lake.

Tom stumbled toward them and crouched as well. "Car engine got shot up… He's out front headed after me… We need to take the boat…" Tom spoke between gasping breaths.

Her thoughts reeled as her heartbeat drummed in her ears. "The other man and Luke are on the lake side of the lodge." How were they going to let Luke know which way they'd gone? They couldn't leave without him.

A shot came through the window that faced the front yard.

"He's advancing on us," said the marshal. "Let's go."

The marshal moved ahead of her toward the door that led to the firepit and the lake. Tom was bent over from the pain. She wrapped her arm around his back to support him.

The marshal crouched and eased the door open. He waited for a second before going outside. He advanced to the firepit. Jillian and Tom slipped outside. The man with the rifle would for sure come through the lodge and follow them.

They didn't have much time. Tom had already made it to the firepit where the marshal was.

Where was Luke? There had been no further shots fired on this side of the lodge.

She hurried toward the firepit and pressed close to the metal. The marshal peered in one direction, and she looked in the other but didn't see anything.

Without saying anything, the marshal crouched and moved toward the lake. Tom followed. Jillian studied the darkness a moment longer before heading toward where the boats were.

She could hear the water lapping against the shore as she drew closer. After lifting the tarp off the boat, the marshal holstered his weapon and helped Tom get in. The boat rocked as she put her foot in.

"We have to wait for Luke," she said

"Call him," whispered the marshal. "Advise him of the plan."

It was a big risk. The phone ringing might put Luke in danger if either attacker was stalking him and close enough to hear. Texting would mean there would be a delay in him seeing the message if he had time to read it at all. She pulled her phone out and pressed his number.

"Yes."

Relief spread through her at the sound of his voice. "We're all at the boats. You need to get here."

She could see the man with the rifle stepping through the sliding glass door and pivoting back and forth. Heart racing, she shut her phone off so the glow of the screen wouldn't give them away.

They all lay flat in the boat. The tarp partially hid them but if the attacker came close enough, he'd see them.

To start the engine now would give them away. She wasn't leaving without Luke.

Please, God, help Luke to get here alive. Protect us all, so we can escape.

When she lifted her head above the rim of the boat, she saw the man with the rifle heading down the hill right toward them.

Luke worried that Jillian had hung up because of imminent danger. At least now, he knew where she was. Would she be able to stay by the boats? Surely, she must know she could leave without him, and he could take another boat. In his attempts to get a jump on the man with the rifle, he'd come across Tom's car and found that it wouldn't start. One of the shooters must have disabled it.

The man he'd taken the handgun off must have had another one in his vehicle and had been stalking him around the property. They'd ended up at the front of the lodge. Luke had taken refuge behind a shed. He angled his body around the corner and peered out, grateful that the night vision goggles revealed the moving shadow in human form and the glint of metal from a gun.

He made a run for the side of the lodge. A single shot zinged through the air, and he slammed against the outside wall. He could see part of the lake but not the dock where the boats were.

He ran to the edge of the lodge. A boat motor started up. He headed down the hill. The boat had just begun to move. Shots were fired at him from the side. This time from a rifle. Luke fired back even as he kept running.

One of the boats moved away from the dock. The night vision goggles allowed him to see the three people in the boat. They'd all made it. He fired another shot toward the firepit, where the man with the rifle was trying to keep him at bay, to give Jillian and the others a fighting chance to get away.

He dove behind the wood pile and then sprinted the remaining distance to the water's edge. The boat was moving very slowly.

When he peered over his shoulder, both men were closing in.

"Luke!" Jillian cried out as she held her hand out toward him.

A rifle shot resounded around him. He stepped into the water and swam. His hand found hers. The boat sped up. Tom was at the helm. Jillian and the marshal pulled Luke into the boat. Jillian wrapped her arms around him.

"You made it." Though he was soaking wet, she drew him close. "I was so afraid for you."

"Get down in the boat," said the marshal.

She let go of him, and they both ducked beneath the rim of the vessel facing in the direction of the shore.

"Jillian, you could've left without me," he whispered. "You all didn't need to risk your lives for me."

"We couldn't leave without you, Luke. I would have stayed behind and let the other two go if it came to that."

Her words were like a soft breeze in the midst of a hurricane. Did she care that much about him?

A rifle shot was fired from the shore. They all ducked even lower in the boat. As they gained speed, Luke heard the rumble of another engine starting up.

Tom steered out into open water.

"Tom, what's the fastest way to get to land and get some more law enforcement help to catch these guys?" Luke spoke above the noise of the motor.

"Plenty of places to go ashore, but it's all wilderness and a few cabins," said Tom.

The other boat was gaining on them. Luke had to come up with a viable plan.

Handguns would only be effective at close range. The surging of the water and the rocking of the boat might make it harder for the rifleman to make an accurate shot. They were all still bent low in the boat.

His big fear was that the rifleman might try to take out their outboard motor, which would make them vulnerable.

"Tom, maybe make it hard for that guy to hit our motor."

"You got it," said Tom. He steered the boat in a curving snakelike pattern. "I'm going to try to shake these guys." He veered toward what looked like an inlet so suddenly that they all jerked with the movement.

As the boat bumped over the water, Luke saw that they had gone into a place where the lake narrowed. The forest butted up against the shore on two sides.

The marshal spoke up, addressing Tom. "There must be some way for us to contact the forest service. Some way to get some extra manpower."

"I agree." Luke could no longer hear the other motor, though he knew they would be followed. "There's got to be a way to take these guys into custody."

Tom didn't answer right away. "My phone with my contacts in it is back at the lodge."

Though faint, the sound of the other boat

reached Luke's ears. They didn't have much time to come up with a plan.

Tom spoke up. "There's a place to dock not too far from here and a forest service cabin that is a short hike from there. No guarantees that anyone will be there."

"Sounds like our best option," said Luke. Maybe they could find a way to ambush the two men once they were on land. He noticed that the marshal was holding one of his arms close to his body. He knew he'd been injured in the car crash.

Tom sped up as the boat bumped over the water. Luke slid his night vision goggles down over his eyes. The other boat was still behind them. He could see the silhouettes of both men. The man with the rifle crouched at the bow of the boat.

The lake opened back up and one of the shorelines became farther away. A chill breeze ruffled his hair as he kept his gun at the ready.

When he drew his attention to the front of the boat, he could see a dock in the distance.

Tom brought the boat in. It was clear from the stiffness of his movements that Tom was still in pain. Luke jumped up on the pier and tied the boat off. He reached a hand out to help his friend, who groaned and pressed his hand against his side as he stepped ashore. Jillian climbed out of the boat with the marshal following. He, too, seemed to be in a weakened state. His hand was disabled, and he had cuts and bruises on his face.

Luke turned toward Tom. "How far away is the cabin?"

"Just up the hill." Tom's breathing was ragged.

Luke rested his hand on his friend's shoulder. "Can you hold on?"

Tom nodded, but Luke couldn't let go of his concern about his friend.

Luke and Marshal Stiller holstered their weapons in order to climb the steep hill. They needed to keep up the pace. The other boat hadn't been far behind. The uphill trail was a bit overgrown with plant life but still evident. Once the two men saw where they'd docked, it would be easy enough for them to figure out where the four had gone.

Luke wasn't sure if they were in the best position to deal with two armed shooters sent by the mafia, but they had no choice. This was the only way to play offense instead of just running. Their intent was to kill Jillian—to silence her once and for all. He needed to take the two men into custody before they caught her.

EIGHTEEN

Jillian allowed the marshal and then Tom to step in front of her on the trail while Luke pulled his gun and took up the rear. The trail was steep. Before they had rounded the first curve and the brush and trees hid the dock, she heard the noise of the other boat approaching. She'd gone only a few more paces before the noise stopped. The armed men were already at the dock.

Would they even make it to the cabin before the men caught up with them? Would they find help there?

Luke glanced over his shoulder.

The steepness of the trail was making Jillian short of breath. She couldn't imagine how hard it was for Tom. All the same, they picked up the pace even more.

The land leveled off, and the cabin came into view. Once off the narrow trail, they spread out and ran toward the cabin. Luke got to the door first. He opened the unlocked door and stepped aside so Tom and Marshal Stiller could go in first.

Jillian glanced down the hill. Even though there was some moonlight, the thick brush concealed where the men were on the trail. Her heartbeat kicked into high gear as she stepped inside.

Luke closed the door and secured it with the bar that kept it locked from the inside. He ran toward one of the windows that faced the trail. Marshal Stiller moved toward a window on the other side of the cabin. His face had drained of color, and he was still trying to catch his breath. The car crash and the ensuing pursuit had exhausted him.

She fought off the despair that settled around her when she saw that no one was inside. The cabin was single room with a cot, woodstove and foldout camp chair. The clothes on the bed, canned goods and books beside the chair indicated that someone was staying here even if they weren't here now.

Jillian reached a hand toward the woodstove. Even without touching it, she could feel the heat rising up from it. Whoever was staying here had only recently left. Maybe a ranger doing some sort of research in the forest. The cabins were sometimes rented out by civilians as well.

She moved toward a wall by the cot away from the two windows. If shots were fired, they would come through the windows. Her heart was pounding by the time she lowered herself to the floor and leaned her back against the log wall.

Tom moved toward some built-in shelving where there was a radio. He lifted the microphone and spoke into it. "Can anyone hear me?"

No response.

"We're at the forest service cabin of the west inlet of Big Sky Lake. We're in trouble."

Still no answer. Tom's words sank into her psyche.

Luke didn't take his eyes off the window. "Tom, get down."

Tom lifted the radio from the shelf and placed it on the floor. He winced as he eased himself down.

Luke moved away from the window but then slid the goggles over his eyes and lifted his head above the sill. He ran to the other window that faced the trail. "I don't see either man anywhere. They must have made it up here by now."

"I think our other guy with the handgun might be out there in the trees that are closer to the cabin." The hand that Marshal Stiller held his gun in was shaking. "Not sure, though. Lot of trees out there."

The darkness probably didn't allow him to see much. When they'd walked up the trail, the moon had been partially covered by clouds. Jillian's stomach clenched. They gunmen might be on both sides of them. Had this been a mistake?

The cabin provided cover. Staying in the boat had left them exposed. Certainly, the men outside would not advance on the cabin knowing that three men inside had guns.

She glanced in Luke's direction. He lifted his chin. "We got this, Jillian." He must have picked up on her fear.

The marshal moved back and forth between two windows, shaking his head each time he peered out.

No shots were fired. What were the two shooters planning?

Just sitting here wasn't helping her anxiety. She had to do something. She glanced around the room and noticed a basket that contained aspirin and other first aid items under the cot. She crawled toward it, pulled it out and opened it. She drew it closer to her face to see in the dim room. She pulled out a packet that contained painkillers and crawled toward Tom. She handed it to him, then looked over at the marshal. His bent fingers needed to be splinted. He wasn't going to stop to let her do that.

"Thanks," said Tom.

She lifted her head to study the items on the

shelves. "There should be some water around here."

"I can just swallow it dry." Tom tore the packet open.

She might be able to help him even more. "Can you tell me the extent of your injuries? You were badly beaten?"

"Kicked my ribs once I was on the ground." Tom let out breath. "You talk like a nurse."

Luke tilted his head in their direction even while he kept watching out the window.

Tom's comment was a reminder of the reason she'd ended up in this perilous situation. She'd had a full life somewhere long ago and far from here, but she'd loved the wrong man. She'd built a life in Spring Meadow, and that was gone too. Her future, if she lived to see it, was still hanging in the balance.

Luke piped up. "Jillian's had a little bit of medical training, is all."

She appreciated him jumping in with a vague comment to cover her. All the same, Tom stared at her for a long moment.

Tom drew the radio to his mouth. "Can anyone hear me? We're at the west inlet cabin."

The radio crackled and a voice came through. "This is Ranger Stevenson. That's my cabin."

Tom locked eyes with Luke before speaking into the radio. "Where are you?"

"On the north shore by Silo Rock. I'm doing some research on the habits of nocturnal animals. What's going on?"

"We're under siege at your cabin."

"I'm armed," came Ranger Stevenson's voice. "I can get to you. I'm about an hour away by car."

Luke rushed across the floor and took the radio. "How far are we from you by boat?"

"Twenty minutes."

Tom said, "I know where he's at."

Luke spoke into the radio. "I'm concerned you won't get here in time, and I don't want to risk you being shot by the armed men. We'll come to you."

"I can stay put," said the ranger.

"Sounds good." Luke handed the radio back to Tom. Luke spoke to the room. "We need to get out of here as fast as we can."

Marshal Stiller's body jerked. "I see him."

A second later, a shot was fired through the window and then another. The marshal fired back with his left hand. Then he pressed his back against the wall. A sheen of sweat had formed on his forehead, and he still held his right arm close to his body.

More shots were fired.

As the gunfire surrounded her, Jillian pressed against the log wall of the cabin and pulled her knees up to her chest. Taking in a breath to quell her rising fear. How were they going to escape?

Luke moved from one window to the next. "The guy with the rifle is advancing on us." He lifted his gun as though to fire but then lowered his arm, shaking his head. "I've got to get closer to at least hold him off."

Was Luke thinking about leaving the protection of the cabin?

Luke glanced around the room and at the marshal before letting his gaze rest on Jillian.

"No one is watching the front door. Tom, get Jillian down to the boat. Stiller and I are going to try to take these guys in."

A lump formed in Jillian's throat. She wanted to protest but knew it would be useless. Luke had made his choice. He was willing to sacrifice his life to save hers.

Tom was already moving across the floor on all fours so as not to be seen through the window. Jillian moved toward Luke, planting a quick kiss on his cheek.

He gripped her arm. "Wait five minutes. If we're not there or you see us coming, take off. Tom will get you to a safe place."

She nodded and kissed him again. This time on the lips. His knuckles touched her cheek briefly like the brush of butterfly wings.

Tom waited for her by the door. Feeling as

though she were crumbling from the inside out, Jillian scrambled across the floor. She didn't want to leave Luke. This might be the last time she ever saw him.

Luke kept his gaze out the window while he spoke to Tom. "Make sure those guys haven't changed position with a view to that door."

Holding his gun, Tom nodded as he eased the door open, then slipped outside and rose to his feet but stayed close to the wall. After a moment, he waved Jillian out. Her feet touched the well-trod dirt outside the door as her gaze bounced everywhere. Nothing moved, not even the stirring of birds or a breeze.

Tom tugged on her sleeve.

They sprinted the short distance to the trees and brush where the trailhead was. They made their way down the path as fast as they could. Tom let her go in front. She stopped when he lagged behind.

"Keep going," he said.

The dock came into view just as the first volley of shots exploded above them. Luke and the marshal must have stepped out of the cabin. Her heart squeezed tight, but she resisted the urge to run back up the hill.

Putting the gun in his waistband, Tom brushed past her and got into the boat. She walked to where the boat was tied to a post, untied it and tossed the rope inside. Tom reached a hand out for her. She stepped into the boat. More shots were fired up the hill. She cringed each time the silence was shattered by gunfire.

Tom pulled the cord to start the engine, but he let go of it midpull and gripped his rib cage.

"Let me do it," she said. It took her three tries, but the engine fired to life. Tom moved toward the motor so he could steer.

Jillian turned back and stared up the hill, where it had grown silent.

Tom put his hand on her shoulder and spoke above the sputter of the motor. "We can't wait but a minute longer."

After nearly being shot at, Luke had taken shelter behind some brush. The marshal slipped in beside him out of breath and wheezing in air.

Luke peered through the night vision goggles for any sign of movement.

The marshal was in rough shape. There was no way they could take these guys without ending up dead. "Let's get down that hill," said Luke.

They holstered their weapons and bolted toward the trailhead. A single shot was fired in their direction. The men knew where they'd gone. Luke nearly slid down the steeper parts of the trail. The marshal was several paces behind him.

He could hear the sputter of the boat engine as

they came out into the open. The boat was about ten feet from the shore but idling.

"Luke!" Jillian called out to him.

Luke glanced at the other boat, pulled his gun and shot at the motor. The ping of a bullet hitting metal reached his ears. Hopefully they'd just bought time by disabling the other boat's engine.

He ran into the water up to his waist. Jillian held both hands out toward him and pulled him in. He turned to help the marshal in as he waded toward them.

Tom sped up while the marshal held on to the rim of the boat and Jillian and Luke pulled him in. The two assailants had made it to the shore. The man with sniper skills lined up a shot while the other started the boat. Luke's bullet must not have done enough damage to disable to motor.

"Get down," Luke shouted.

Tom increased his speed as the lake opened up. Luke had no idea where they were going, but Tom seemed to have a plan.

Jillian's hand found his and she squeezed it. "I'm glad you made it," she whispered close to his ear.

"Me too," he said. "I only wish that I could have taken those guys in."

"At least we got away," said Jillian.

When he peered through the night vision goggles, he could see the other boat some distance behind them. If he'd done any damage at all to the engine, it hadn't been enough to completely disable it. The other vessel, though it remained in sight, didn't seem to be gaining speed.

Tom maneuvered the boat around a rocky island. Up ahead, he saw a tree-covered peninsula that jutted out into the lake and by it a rock that looked like a silo.

"The ranger's just over there." Tom pointed.

They skimmed through the water. Through the goggles, Luke saw light and then a car came into view. When he looked over his shoulder, the other boat was still behind them.

Not close enough to shoot at them, but definitely close enough to see where they were going.

NINETEEN

Jillian glanced at Tom as he brought the boat into the rocky shoreline. The two attackers were still following them.

Luke jumped out and pulled the boat closer to shore. He helped Jillian out, and then the two of them aided the injured men.

Tom pointed at the rocky incline. "Just up this way."

They'd climbed only for a few minutes before Ranger Stevenson came into view holding a flashlight. He helped them up the remainder of the hill.

His SUV with the ranger insignia on it sat in a flat area surrounded by trees. "I've already packed up my equipment." The ranger shone the flashlight toward Tom and Marshal Stiller but not in their eyes. "It looks like you could use some medical attention."

They walked toward the vehicle.

The ranger opened one of the back doors.

"Gonna be a little cramped, but I'll get you to a clinic."

They climbed into the car. Luke sat beside her in the back seat by the window after he helped Tom in. The marshal was up front with the ranger.

The sun was just beginning to come up as they drove along the road that ran parallel to the lake. When Jillian looked out toward the water, she saw the boat with the two men in the distance.

"I see them." Luke patted her leg, then said to the ranger, "Can you radio the position of that boat out there? The men who tried to kill us are in it. See if we can get some law enforcement out to catch them."

The ranger glanced through his window. "Sure. I'll advise the forest service of the location and direction of travel. They can get a boat out there."

Tom had fallen asleep resting his head against the window. The ranger's voice became background noise to her own thoughts. Maybe the two men would be taken into custody. That didn't mean things were over for her. She took comfort in sitting close to Luke. His proximity calmed her. For now, they were together.

About a half hour later, they arrived at a small town that consisted of a few homes, a post office and a café/convenience store that, judging from the ads in the window, sold mostly camping supplies. The ranger slowed his SUV and parked in front of a clinic that was separated from the other buildings. The building looked dark.

The ranger pushed open the door. "Doc lives in the back of building. He's used to doing triage for hikers and hunters. I might be getting him out of bed, but he'll fix you up nice."

The four of them got out of the SUV and walked toward the entrance. A few minutes later, the door opened and a bleary-eyed man with ginger hair and a beard, wearing what looked like hastily thrown-on jeans and a hoodie, opened the door. The ranger was behind him.

The man held out his hand. "I'm Doctor Grayson. I hear you folks need some tending to."

Jillian stepped to one side and tilted her head toward the marshal. "His fingers need to be splinted." She touched Tom's back. "His ribs may be bruised or even broken. Both of them could use some strong pain medication until they can get further treatment."

She sounded like a nurse and she didn't care. She was beat up and worn out and so very tired of having to be on the run.

The doctor stared at her for a moment. "Definitely." He reached a hand toward the marshal. "Right this way. I'll take you first." He pointed at Tom. "There's a second exam room down the hall if you want to get into a gown. I don't have an X-ray machine, but I can maybe wrap your rib cage after I take a look."

Holding his arms close to his body, Tom stumbled down the hall. The ranger stood by the door. "I suppose I need to arrange for some transport for you folks."

"Yes," said Luke. "If Tom doesn't need further medical treatment, he needs a ride back to his fishing lodge. Given the marshal's condition, I think I'll be going with him and Jillian."

She and Luke would not be saying goodbye at least for a while longer.

"I can take Tom home or for further medical treatment if needed," Stevenson said. "I'll get on my radio and see what I can do about acquiring a vehicle for the three of you." The ranger stepped outside. He hadn't asked any questions, though he'd probably figured out that Jillian was under protection and in the middle of a transport.

Jillian and Luke sat alone in the small waiting room, which consisted of four hard plastic chairs and a counter.

She put her hand on his where it rested on his knee. "I thought for sure you were going to die at the cabin." Her throat had gone tight, and she could no longer hold back the flood of emotions. Tears rolled down her cheeks.

He wrapped an arm around her and drew her into a sideways hug.

Her crying was partly over all they had been through but more so because of the knowledge that she and Luke would have to part ways. It caused intense sorrow.

As she bent her head and wept, he rubbed her back. She relished the safety of being close to him, of feeling his comforting touch even if she knew it wouldn't last.

By the time the ranger stepped back into the waiting room, she was all cried out and had grabbed a tissue from a box on a nearby table to wipe her eyes.

"Car is on its way. It's the junker we use to go up into the high mountains. It runs fine, but it's nothing to look at. Another ranger is bringing it. He'll ride with me and Tom."

"Wonderful," said Luke. "We'll figure out a way to get it returned to you." He rose to his feet and held his hand out to the ranger. "Thanks for everything."

Stevenson gave Luke's upper arm two slaps. "Glad to do it. One thing you need to be aware of. While I was talking with my colleague, a call came over the radio that the man we sent to look for that boat couldn't find it."

"So, those two men are still at large?" Luke turned to look at Jillian as the ranger nodded.

The news put her on edge. Still, how would

the shooters know where they'd gone once they were on the way to the safe house?

They waited a few more minutes, and the marshal emerged with his fingers splinted and wrapped. Luke explained the plan to him.

The marshal nodded as he sat down. He lifted his injured hand. "I'm not in the best kind of shape to fend off an attack. I made a call to have a local law enforcement officer meet me at the safe house, but it will be good to have you along for the transport, Luke."

A few minutes later, Tom emerged from the hallway. Once the second car showed up, they congregated outside.

Jillian gave Tom a gentle hug. "Thank you for everything."

"Glad to help a friend," said Tom.

While Jillian stepped to one side and stood by the marshal, Luke patted his friend's back. "I'll make sure you get payment for damages to your place and boat."

"I know you're good for it. Take care of yourself, Luke." He glanced over at Jillian. "And her."

"Take care, my friend." While Tom stood close, Luke turned to face Marshal Stiller. "Where are we headed?"

"House just outside of Merrisville," Stiller said.

They all waved one final goodbye to Tom as he got into the SUV with the two rangers. Luke slipped behind the wheel with the marshal in the passenger seat. Jillian sat in the middle of the back seat.

Within a half hour, they were off the forest roads and back on the highway. As they got closer to the safe house, Jillian felt a heaviness sink into her bones. Soon, she would be out of Montana and headed toward her new life.

The marshal was talking on the phone and turned sideways to look at her. "We might have you placed into your new location within a few days."

This was it then. She'd be learning a new cover and starting a new life somewhere else. Her voice came out in a monotone. "Where will I be going?"

"Looking at setting you up in either in a rural town in Washington state or outside Chicago."

Jillian sat back in her seat and watched the landscape go by in a blur.

"I promised Jillian we'd figure out a way to get her cats to her." Luke's voice sounded soft and far away.

"We'll see what we can do," said Marshal Stiller. "Maybe arrange for them to be transported on the plane when she leaves."

Jillian felt like they were talking about her as if she weren't even in the car. Part of her had gone numb to keep from feeling the pain over leaving her life behind. This time was harder. When she'd left New Jersey, it was the job and friends she was going to miss. But there'd been a degree of relief that she would no longer be frequenting all the places that reminded her of how blind she'd been when she'd fallen in love with Gregory.

Why was this time so much harder? Why did it hurt so much more?

Luke slowed once they were inside the city limits of Merrisville. Marshal Stiller recited the address. Luke drove through town past several blocks of shops with homes behind them. Minutes later, he pulled up in front of a mobile home with a chain-link fence around it.

"No garage?" Luke turned the engine off.

"This is the best we could do on short notice that was driving distance from Spring Meadow. The place is far enough from other homes that we won't have any nosy neighbors who might talk. Like I said, I'm going to get Jillian out of here as quickly as I can."

She saw only one other house that had to be at least two blocks away. A storage unit and an appliance repair shop that looked closed were on the other side of the street, which became a dirt road not too far from the trailer. A dense forest stood behind the trailer.

The three of them got out of the car.

Luke looked over at her. "I'll walk you to the

door. Make sure you're safe inside." The warmth she saw in his eyes made her heart flutter.

"Actually—" the marshal looked up from his phone "—the deputy who was supposed to help with protection duty has been delayed. He's coming from an hour away. This little town doesn't have a police force."

"I can stay," said Luke. "Until you have some backup."

"Much appreciated." The marshal pulled a key from his pocket and opened the door for them, allowing Jillian and Luke to go in first.

Luke's words, *I can stay*, bounced around inside Jillian's head. She knew why this new placement was harder than the first one. This time she would be leaving behind someone she loved. Despite how guarded she'd been around him out of fear that she'd lost the ability to see someone's true character, her feelings for him had grown as she witnessed over and over his kindness and courage. His willingness to protect her life at the risk of his own had made her realize that she loved him.

As she stepped inside, she looked at him. He was already moving through the living room and kitchen and peering out windows. He stopped and glanced in her direction as a soft smile spread across his face, making his eyes light up.

Maybe he had feelings for her as well. It didn't

matter. The situation was impossible. She'd keep her realization to herself. He'd already suffered enough heartache and loss in his life.

"I better check the place out. Get a feel for the layout." Luke's hand touched her arm as he brushed past her and headed down the hallway.

The marshal opened the fridge. "This was supposed to be stocked. Looks like we got a few things in here. Are you hungry?"

Jillian chose the chair in the living room that was away from any windows. Force of habit now. She hadn't eaten since being at the lodge. It was well past breakfast now. Food didn't sound good to her though. "I can wait."

Though the trailer was a bit rundown, the few pieces of furniture looked like it had been bought off the showroom floor, and everything matched.

The marshal handed her a bottled water. "At least drink this."

He retreated to the other side of the trailer, where the master suite must be. Luke came back up the hallway and sat down.

The marshal returned shortly after. "I'll get a feel for what we have around us." He stepped outside.

Placing his gun on a side table, Luke sat down opposite her.

"Here we go again, huh?" she said.

He cleared his throat. "What do you mean?"

She picked up a book from a stack on the side table by the chair. "You standing guard over me, protecting me." She looked up from the book she'd flipped open. His eyes had depth enough to get lost in. "This will be the last time. You'll go back to Spring Meadow after this." What emotion did she read in those eyes, the sideways tilt of his head and furrowing of his brow? Sadness maybe?

"Yes, going to be some changes though." He pulled his gaze from her and stared out a window. "I told Matt to get the ball rolling on selling the farm."

She let out a breath. She hadn't expected that. "Luke, that's a big transition for you. I think it will be good for you and your family though."

"You helped me see why I was holding on to it." He smiled in a way that sent a charge of electricity through her. "I am forever grateful to you for that, Jillian, who helps everyone."

His phone rang, interrupting the moment. He stood up and turned away from her. "Tom…? What is it? Slow down." Luke paced the room and reached down for his gun while still holding the phone.

Fear lanced through her at the tone of Luke's voice.

Something had happened to Tom.

TWENTY

Luke's friend sounded frantic. "I'm at the lodge. I've called the police."

"What happened?" Luke asked. "What are you saying?"

"Those men came back here. They forced me to say where you were going. Luke, I'm so sorry. They would have killed me if I hadn't."

"Are you okay?"

"I'm alive. That's what matters."

"We're an hour away from you. We have time to get Jillian moved out of here."

Tom huffed out a breath. "Luke, they knocked me unconscious. I just came to. It's been at least an hour already. I called you right after I called the police."

Luke's heart pounded in his chest. The two men couldn't know the exact address, but this was a small town that would take only a short time to drive through. "Do they know what kind of car we were driving?" The junker would be easy to spot.

"Yes, unfortunately. I'm so sorry." Tom's voice sounded so small.

"Don't be. You've been through enough to win friend of the year." Before he even said goodbye to Tom, Luke was headed toward the door that led outside. They needed to hide that distinct car.

Jillian had gotten to her feet. He glanced back at her as he pushed the door open.

"They've found us, haven't they?" Her eyes were wide with fear.

"Yes."

"I'll go to the bedroom and stay on the floor out of sight." She retreated down the hall.

Before he could step outside, the marshal pushed through the door. "Suspicious car just went by. Going slow and staring at this place. How would they even know where to look?"

Luke clenched his teeth. They were already here and had spotted the car and maybe the marshal. "Got a call from Tom. They tortured the answer out of him."

Luke peered out the window at the empty road. "Which way were they headed?"

"Drove toward that storage unit." Marshal Stiller pointed. "Haven't come back this way."

The marshal was still dealing with a useless shooting hand. "You watch the living room," Luke said. "I'll go stay with Jillian. How soon until that deputy gets here?"

"Last text said he was about twenty minutes out."

Jillian could be dead by then if they didn't make the right choices.

The marshal pulled his gun, taking up a position by the window. Luke hurried down the hall. Jillian sat in the corner of the room with her knees pulled up to her chest. The panic and vulnerability on her face tied his stomach into knots.

He leaned over and patted her shoulder.

After resting her hand on his, she tilted her head. "I'm so glad you're here with me."

The look in her eyes and the tone of her voice, something had shifted between them. He wanted to say that there was no other place that he would rather be, even under these circumstances, but the words got caught in his throat. Why give her false hope? If they got out of this alive, they'd part ways.

Pulling his hand free of hers, he turned his attention to the room.

The bedroom had windows on both sides that provided a view of the front and back of the property. He watched the trees that bordered the back yard before looking out the window that faced the road. He didn't see either man approaching.

The marshal was calling him on the phone. "No sign of the car coming back," Stiller said in a low voice.

"I suspect they parked by the storage unit to hide the car and move in on foot," Luke responded.

"I don't think they know I spotted them. I was just coming around the side of the house when the car went by," said the marshal.

Luke moved back over to the window that faced the forest. "Hard to say what they have planned."

"Some sort of psychological waiting game?" Stiller offered. "Hoping we try to leave or make some kind of stupid move."

"Past behavior tells me that they'll be strategic." Luke leaned closer to the window, still not seeing any movement in the trees.

There was a narrow field of overgrown grass between the forest and the back of the trailer. An old washing machine knocked on its side, along with several other appliances stacked on top of each other, sat in the grass. A few feet away was a pile of tires that someone could hide behind.

"Time is on our side," said the marshal. "If they delay making a move, the deputy might get here to help us out."

Luke honed in on the washing machine wondering if a man was crouched behind it. "Did you let the deputy know what he was walking into?"

"Just talked to him. He's prepared."

Luke stayed on the line as he checked out the window that faced the road again.

"I saw one of them," said the marshal. Then the line went dead.

A second later a single shot was fired from the living room. The bedroom window shattered, and something landed on the floor. A grenade.

Adrenaline surged through Luke.

He swept Jillian up and ran toward the hallway just as the explosion happened behind them. A force like a hot board being slapped against his back pushed their bodies up the hallway as debris rained down around them. They both landed on their stomachs. His skin felt like it was on fire as he grabbed the back of Jillian's coat and lifted her up to keep running.

Both men must be close to the trailer. What if they had another grenade? Not a chance they could take. The man with the rifle appeared to be well trained and well-armed, probably ex-military.

The marshal was already headed toward the back door when they got to the living room. Luke guided Jillian toward the door right behind the marshal. They burst outside and headed toward the trees. When a gunshot resounded behind them, the marshal took refuge behind the tires, and Jillian and Luke dove for the piled-up appliances. Jillian pressed in close to him in order to be completely hidden.

Luke peered out from behind the washing

machine but didn't see either man. At least one of them must be pressed against the side of the trailer, looking for a chance to fire another shot.

Judging from the sound, the shot had come from a handgun, not a rifle. The trees were a better place to hide. They had to make a run for it. The guy with the handgun would have to move in closer to get a decent shot. Luke would be ready for him. His only concern was that the guy with the rifle would be coming after them or he had another grenade he could utilize. Best to get out of here before the rifleman had a chance to shoot at them.

He whispered to Jillian. "You go." He pointed toward the forest. "I'll hold him off."

Fear clouded her face. She leaned close and kissed him. She turned and worked her way toward the trees. He didn't have to tell her to stay low and to move in a line, so the appliances hid her from view as long as possible.

He leaned back to get a look at the marshal signaling as to what his plan was. Luke pointed back toward the other side of the trailer communicating that the marshal should try to flank the shooter. Jillian had crawled halfway across the field when the man with the handgun came around the corner. The marshal took off toward the other side of the trailer.

Luke lifted his head, fired a shot and hunched

back down. The shooter retreated to the safety of the side of the trailer. A flash of movement drew Luke's attention to the inside of the trailer. The rifleman had taken up a position by a window.

Jillian made it to the safety of the forest before the rifleman could fire a shot at her. The marshal disappeared around the corner of the trailer. Hoping to create a distraction, Luke ran toward the tires.

The sniper fired a shot at him that glanced off the tires. How long would it take the marshal to get around the trailer? Had he seen the rifleman inside before he ran around the corner?

Luke listened to the sound of his own breathing. The rifleman stepped away from the window. Where was he going now?

He looked off to the side by the forest. At least fifty yards away, Jillian had come out from the safety of the trees, headed across the road and sprinted toward the storage unit. What was she doing?

He waited a second, thinking the man with the handgun would step out and pursue her. When he didn't, Luke ran out in the open, ready to shoot as he passed the side of the trailer. The man was no longer there.

Two shots, one right after the other, were fired from the front of the trailer. Luke hurried around in time to see the man with the handgun from the back. His gun was still held in a shooting position. He must have been firing at the marshal.

"Drop the gun. Hands up!" Luke yelled.

The man complied. Luke moved in closer but didn't see the marshal anywhere. Had he been hit?

Luke advanced toward the shooter. He had no way to restrain him.

"Marshal?" Luke called.

"Yeah." The reply from the side of the trailer was weak.

"Could use your handcuffs," said Luke. He looked toward the trailer, kept his gun on the shooter and wondered what the rifleman was up to. Had he heard the interaction?

The marshal emerged from the side of the mobile home where part of the wall was missing from the grenade detonating. He advanced toward Luke, glancing side to side.

Luke took the cuffs. "Were you hit?"

Marshal Stiller shook his head. "Just out of breath."

Luke spoke to the shooter. "Hands down and behind your back." He slapped the cuffs on him and secured them. Finally, they had one of the attackers. Now to catch the other.

"Lay on the ground and don't move." Luke waited until the man was on his stomach. He bent over him. "What's your partner up to?"

"I don't know. I'm not his partner." The man lifted his head slightly. "I'm from Spring Meadow. He hired me to help him. I met him at the hotel I work at." Luke's mind reeled. Stanley Reese had left town, but the second suspect they thought might be the stalker... "I don't suppose he goes by the name Jon Wilson?"

"Yeah, but that's not his real name."

Up the road, he saw the deputy's patrol vehicle kicking up dust as it drew nearer. Luke took in a breath. They had one man in custody and help was on the way.

From above him, he heard the zing of rifle shots. The patrol vehicle slowed and then stopped all together.

The sniper had taken up a position on top of the trailer. Both the marshal and Luke pressed against the wall of the mobile home, leaving the restrained man lying on the ground.

The deputy got out of the SUV holding his handgun and pressing close to the car. Another shot was fired in his direction. The deputy retreated to the back of the vehicle.

Luke's phone made a dinging sound. A text?

When he looked at it, he saw it was from Jillian.

This time I'm the distraction.

Luke could barely process what she meant when he saw the assailant's car emerge from behind the storage unit and head toward the trailer but going slow.

"I need to get on the roof," he whispered to the marshal. There was no way the marshal could climb with one bad hand.

Shots were fired at the car Jillian was in. The windshield shattered. He couldn't see Jillian behind the wheel anymore. His heart squeezed tight and he prayed she had ducked down below the dashboard and not been hit.

The deputy had begun to move in closer. He must have seen that the sniper's attention was on Jillian. Luke knew he couldn't wait for the deputy to get here.

No more bullets flew, and the car remained motionless. Luke still couldn't see Jillian behind the wheel. He wiped the thought that something bad had happened to her from his mind.

Focus on the mission.

As the deputy moved in, Luke ran inside the trailer and advanced toward the open window that the rifleman must have used to get on the roof. After holstering his weapon so he could use both hands, he pulled himself through the window, trying to be as quiet as possible.

Another shot was fired from the roof. He cringed. Then he heard the stomping of feet above him and more gunfire. Luke reached up for the rim of the trailer and hauled himself up.

The rifleman's back was to him. Judging from the way he was positioned, he was taking aim at the deputy.

Because it would take two hands to maneuver, Luke wouldn't be able to pull his weapon until he was fully on the roof.

A shot came from off to the side. In his peripheral vision, he could see that the marshal had climbed up on the dryer that was upright to take the shot that would distract the rifleman. The marshal jumped behind the dryer just as Luke pulled himself up to the roof of the trailer. He pulled his gun before he was even settled.

The rifleman swung around, chambering a round as Luke got to his feet. Another shot came from the side of the house by the appliances. The rifleman glanced in the direction of the shot.

Time enough for Luke to barrel toward him and tackle him. Taking him in alive would answer a lot of questions about who he was. The rifleman fell backward. Luke was on top of him. He punched him across the jaw.

The man fought back, slamming the rifle into Luke's jaw. Because Luke was temporarily stunned from the blow, the sniper was able to get up on his knees. Luke raised his gun to fire.

The man hit him again in the face with the butt of the rifle and then used it to knock Luke's gun out of his hand.

Luke dove at the man, seeking to wrestle the rifle away from him. More shots were fired from down below from the side of the trailer where the deputy was, but at this distance and angle, the bullets couldn't hit their mark.

Luke wrestled the rifle away from the sniper and hit him on the back and shoulder until the man went down to his knees.

Luke stood over him with the rifle aimed at the other man's chest. "Deputy?"

The deputy had crawled through the window the same way Luke had come and had his hands around the rim of the trailer. He pushed himself up. "Yes?"

"Could use a pair of your handcuffs. We'll have to get him down off the roof first."

The deputy and marshal held their guns on the sniper while he crawled down after Luke. The man was then handcuffed, and the deputy led him back to the patrol car.

Luke didn't wait while the marshal made sure the suspect on the ground was secured in the patrol car as well. He ran up the road to where the assailants' car stood. Before he even got to it, he saw Jillian sitting up behind the wheel.

He pulled open the door and gathered her into his arms. She stepped out of the car while he held her. He brushed his hand over her hair. "I was afraid that the bullet had found its target." He held her face in his hands so he could look into her eyes. "And that I'd lost you."

He wanted to say that he loved her because now he knew that he did. The thought of her dying made him realize his true feelings. He couldn't bring himself to say the words. She'd be stepping out of his life and into a new one soon. If she stayed here, the mafia would just send more men. "You didn't have to do that. Risk your life like that."

"Sure, I did. You did it for me more than once." She reached up and rested her palm against his cheek. "And for that I am eternally grateful." She kissed him.

He held her for a long moment even after the kiss ended, knowing it would be the last time.

Jillian sat in the police station where the deputy had taken the two men. Luke and the marshal had been in separate interview rooms with each of the men for well over an hour. She was grateful for the hot cup of coffee that one of the other deputies had brought her.

The ache in her heart was almost unbearable. The immediate threat against her life had been taken care of. All three attackers—Roger, Wilson and his man for hire—had been arrested. But she doubted it meant she could return to Spring Meadow.

Luke emerged from the interview room and sat down beside her on the bench. The marshal sat on the other side of her. Both of them had expressions that looked like they'd been carved in stone.

The marshal spoke first. "We've identified the two men who came after you. The man with the sniper skills is the brother of the hitman you put in jail. He was using the alias Jon Wilson to track you down. He seems to be in the family business of gun for hire and had a military career before taking up the family trade."

"The other guy is a man the sniper met in Spring Meadow," said Luke.

"So maybe it's just Burnett's brother wanting revenge on me? The mafia may not know where I am..."

The marshal shook his head. "The choice is always yours, Jillian. But given that your testimony also put the man who hired the hitman in jail, we still think that your life could be under threat."

"I understand." The men who'd pursued her had been arrested and would face jail time, but the mafia could still find her. She bent her head and stared at the coffee in her hand.

"I've made some calls. I can get you on a plane before the day is over. You can stay at a temporary location until we finalize your new identity."

The marshal cupped his hand on her shoulder. "I'll give you a moment. I'm ready to escort you as soon as you're ready."

She nodded. Jillian stared into her coffee while the marshal walked away. It was time to leave Montana.

Luke shifted in the seat next to her. "I'll see to it that your cats are transported to you."

She took a sip of her coffee, which had grown cold. "Thank you, Luke. For everything."

"We helped each other." He smiled softly. "I think my life will be a lot different once the farm is sold. I wouldn't have been able to move on without your insight into why I was so stuck."

She couldn't bring herself to look into his eyes. Instead she stared straight ahead. "I guess this is it. This is really goodbye."

He leaned a little closer to her so that their shoulders were touching. "You need to do what you have to do to keep yourself safe."

She turned to look at him, searching the depth of his eyes. "Yes, but at what cost? I'll be leaving you." It would be cruel for her to say that she loved him. Not when those would be her final words to him.

He leaned in and kissed her. "You take care of yourself, Jillian."

She didn't want to delay the inevitable any longer. Jillian rose and threw the remainder of the coffee away before walking to the room where the marshal had gone.

She stepped through the open door. Marshal Stiller turned to face her. "You ready?"

She nodded. "Let's get out of here."

TWENTY-ONE

Six Months Later

Jillian secured the pet rabbit in its crate before turning her attention to the dog that was just waking up from anesthesia. She opened the kennel he was in and stroked his head while he licked her hand.

"There you go." She stared at the gauze wrapped around his leg. "Poor thing. I know it doesn't make any sense to you."

It had been six months since she'd come to the town of Riverbend, Washington, with a population of 7,500 people. Her job as an assistant at the vet clinic made her feel like she'd found her niche with work. Helping animals and the people who loved them suited her.

Marmy stayed at the clinic during the day while George remained at home. The job was certainly more fulfilling than what she'd done in Spring Meadow. Yet her thoughts always seemed to turn to the life she had there more often than the life she'd left behind in New Jersey.

She stared out at the snow falling outside after gathering Marmy in her arms from the cat condo where she lounged. Spring would be coming soon. One season would roll into another and this would be her life. She'd made some friends, found a church, gotten to know her neighbors. Once again, she'd build a life for herself.

The receptionist, Anna, poked her head in. "Jillian, there's a guy out here who says his horse is having gastrointestinal issues. The vet is out on an emergency call. Could you answer some of his questions? I'm headed out to lunch."

"Sure." She stepped out into the reception area.

Her breath caught when she saw Luke standing on the other side of the counter. He wore a Western-cut button-down shirt and a cowboy hat. Marmy jumped from her arms and wandered over to rub against Luke's leg.

She cleared her throat, glancing at Anna, who was gathering her purse. "I hear you have a horse with some digestive problems."

Luke shrugged. "She's old, but I am concerned about her."

Anna came around the desk. "See you in an hour." She headed toward the door.

Once the door closed, Jillian rushed over to Luke. "What are you doing here?"

"Don't get upset. I worked with the marshal to ensure that every precaution has been taken to keep you safe."

She was in shock from seeing him. "I still don't understand."

"The farm sold in Spring Meadow. I'm looking at buying an apple orchard not too far from here. I want to be with you, Jillian. I want to be a part of your life."

She shook her head, unable to process what he was saying.

"I'll understand if you think it's too much of a safety risk for you."

"No, that's not what I was worried about. I know you wouldn't put me in danger." Her heart swelled with love for him. In all these months, her feelings for him hadn't changed. "But why are you here?"

He took off his hat and twirled it in his hand. "The last few months without you have been miserable. I missed you so much."

"I missed you too." She knew now why life felt so gray. She wanted to live it with Luke. And she hadn't been able to.

"The marshal is putting together a new identity for me. But the only way that can go through is if we're married." He looked her in the eyes, appearing hopeful but also uncertain.

She put her hands on her hips. "Luke Mayfair. That is like the worst proposal ever."

"I… No. I didn't mean it that way." He ran his hands through his hair and shuffled his feet. "I didn't mean that I only wanted to marry you so I could enter the program." He shuffled his feet. "Sorry, this is coming out all wrong. I know this is a big step. And we don't have much time to decide. It's not fair to you."

"So, you're going to leave your family behind?"

"They're all leaving Spring Meadow. My mom is looking to buy a shop in some other town. Tasha has several teaching offers."

"You're giving up so much. Are you sure you want to do that?"

"It's time I started a new chapter of my life." He held her eyes with his. "I want to be with you, Jillian. I want to be your husband and grow old with you." He pulled a box out from his pocket and flipped it open. "Marry me."

The ring was a simple diamond in a gold setting.

He bent his head, so it was close to hers. "Did I do it right that time?"

Her heart clenched at the sight of him holding the ring out to her. "You've left me breathless."

"So, what's your answer?"

She swatted him on the arm. "Of course I'll marry you."

He put his hat back on his head. "Give me your hand." He pulled the ring out and placed it on her finger.

Feeling weak in the knees and like her head was buzzing, she gazed up at him. "Thank you, Luke. You've made me very happy."

"I got you beat. You've made me ecstatic." He grinned, sweeping her up into his arms and twirling her around before placing her on the floor. He leaned in to kiss her.

When he pulled free of the kiss and touched his palm to her face, Jillian looked into the depths of the eyes. "God has a way of restoring things better than we could have hoped or imagined, doesn't He?"

He took her in his arms again. "Yes, He does."

Jillian relished being held by the man she was going to spend the rest of her life with.

* * * * *

*If you enjoyed this story,
be sure to check out other thrilling titles by
USA TODAY bestselling author
Sharon Dunn.
Available from Love Inspired Suspense!
Discover more at LoveInspired.com.*